PATRICIA BROWNING
GRIFFITH

 The Future
Is Not What It
Used to Be

SIMON AND SCHUSTER, NEW YORK

For Bill

The walls and ceiling of my room are gray—
The moon's color through the windows of a laundromat.
I close my eyes.

. . .

I see myself in the park
on horseback, surrounded by dark,
leading the armies of peace.
The iron legs of the horse do not bend.

I drop the reins. Where will the turmoil end?
Fleets of taxis stall
in the fog, passengers fall
asleep. Gas pours

from a tri-colored stack.
Locking their doors,
people from offices huddle together,
telling the same story over and over.

Everyone who has sold himself wants to buy himself back.
Nothing is done. The night
eats into their limbs
like a blight.

Everything dims.
The future is not what it used to be.
The graves are ready. The dead
shall inherit the dead.

—FROM "The Way It Is" by Mark Strand

Reprinted from *The New York Review of Books,*
© 1968 *The New York Review*

I was born and raised i' the country, Mamma,
but I'm stayin' in town . . .

—HUDDIE LEDBETTER

I

Sunny. Slim, brown-haired, pale. Lying in the damp grass, warm in her wool clothes, drunk with the sun skimming off the gray Potomac, the earth fresh and new green beneath her. A blade of grass stood against her lips. Her arms pressed against the uneven ground over knots of grass, unwarmed dirt, tattered leaves. Now and then she'd open her eyes to follow the silhouette of a jet crossing overhead, its gray trail swelling slowly and disappearing into the crystal sky like an old car speeding down a dusty country road.

Beside her Fletcher. Bronze, pleasant round face, incipient beer belly. Drinking beer. Watching others who'd fled squalid city rooms to drop lines into the oily gray water, or to lie on dark, dirty blankets eating sandwiches from paper sacks while children rolled and ran around the trees and between the cars which were lined up bumper to bumper alongside the road.

It was March and the first warm day of the year. To Sunny Tidwell and Fletcher Conners, the warmth was a liquor to their souls for they were children of summer—of baking unwalkable beaches along the Gulf, of creeping russet falls where some trees held their leaves till Christmas; of quick invigorating winters where a snowfall meant a holiday and everyone taking pictures; of long languid springs and fields of wild flowers beside straight diaphanous highways, of summers that scorched and curdled the earth—southwestern summers observed through the drone of glassed air-conditioned isolation. There the spring and its warmth had been too close, too smothering and constant. Here in the city it was to be sought, savored, marveled at. It came in brief patches and was often half-hearted as this day when the sun began to slide away and Sunny felt the ground cool beneath her and the air chill. They watched as the cars thinned out and the lovers rolled up in their blankets and the transistor radios quieted. Only the planes kept their pace, lifting slowly over the water one after another heading toward similar cities, similar gray waters, crowded parks, tired city-worn people hungry for warmth.

After a while Fletcher stood and languidly Sunny lifted her arms. Fletcher pulled her up, hugging her to him briefly, kissing her neck, and they separated, walking toward the car, Fletcher carrying a cooler, stopping to pull a leaf from Sunny's hair.

The city was clear, fresh, like new. From a height you could see all the way to the Blue Ridge Mountains this afternoon, said a radio announcer.

"That's an occasion," Sunny said.

"Definitely worth celebrating with a beer," Fletcher agreed.

They stopped at Floyd's Restaurant and Go-Go Bar, two blocks from the Capitol, an ugly anachronism where evenings Fletcher, straight from the marble corridors, could tuck his tie into his pocket and escape the dull self-consciousness that predominated the area. And Sunny, estranged congressional daughter, wearing huaraches, could listen to conversations

about love and heartbreak instead of vote counts and commit-
tees. She could watch fat ladies dance and truck drivers make
passes. It was here on New Year's Eve that a forty-seven-year-
old woman with long dyed permanented hair, feeling herself
an anachronism, had cried drunkenly on both Sunny's and
Fletcher's shoulders. It was, Sunny believed, like all the
buildings in the area, haunted by relatives of early politicians.

"I can assure you," she said, "their having lived with a
politician means they were unhappy and are tossing about in
their graves full of unrequited vengeance. Old ghostly Whig
relatives are probably in here drinking every night after Floyd
closes."

They spent the evening drinking beer and watching the
band, one skinny guy on an electric guitar and a fat ex-boxer
on drums, and the go-go girl writhing on the tiny wooden
platform. Alma, the dancer, was a tall dark-haired girl who
wore glasses, except when she danced, and had runners in her
stockings. She did a relatively ladylike go-go which didn't
change much from month to month despite the go-go vogues.
Fletcher once told her she was the most gentle go-go dancer
he'd ever seen. She thanked him and said it was because she
was from North Carolina.

Beside Sunny and Fletcher two plump girls were doing a
vigorous jerk with a couple of hair-shorn marine recruits.

"This is the real world," Sunny announced to Fletcher.

"This is only part of the real world," he corrected.

"Oh, no, it's *the* real," she insisted. "Realer than the other
anyway. The Tidwell dictionary says 'real is a matter of being
without artifice; concerned with basics.'" She tapped her
finger on the table for emphasis.

"And what do you consider basics?" he asked, emptying his
beer into his glass.

She bit her lower lip and stared toward the ceiling trying

not to smile. "Basics are love, sex, back rubs . . . children, animals . . . daydreams, and trees," she said. "Those are good basics. The bad basics are something else, of course, and they aren't as basic as good basics. I guess I'm still an optimist," she said, resting her chin in her hands.

Fletcher leaned toward Sunny in a demonstration of profound fascination, watching her wide mobile face that betrayed her in the slightest untruth. She was no beauty but her face made Fletcher think of Greek drama when he knew little about Greek drama.

"Give me an example of bad basics," Fletcher asked her.

"Bad basics," she explained seriously, "are heavily D's—death, dentists . . . cops, dishes, dreams . . . elevators, and cars."

"Cars!"

She nodded.

"God, that's un-American," he said, then realizing it was a bad subject, changed it. "You left out songs."

"Oh, yes, that's definitely a good basic," she said smiling again.

"You don't think politics is a bad basic?"

"Oh, no, millions of people live without politics, don't you think?"

"No, there's always some power struggle. Where there are two people there's politics."

"You're becoming corrupt," she said.

"Besides, millions live without dentists," he said, ignoring her charge.

"Dentists are just a D for teeth," she said, and they laughed.

The band lunged into a hillbilly number. They shifted between rock-and-roll and country-western. To close observers such as Sunny and Fletcher it was clear, however, that the singer's heart was with the country-western songs. There was a special intensity and tremolo tone that he brought to the country-western songs of lament which were absent from the others. With his long thin face and black oiled hair, his head big for his thin body, his eyes closed, he approached them nostalgically, his voice taking on an unself-conscious anticipation as though he were at a seance and summoning some painful apparition.

> *One has my name . . .*
> *The other has my heart. . . .**

He sang every line with conviction, swaying slightly in the blue light, which gave the room the listless, comforting air of a midnight ocean voyage.

At the bar a woman slept while a barmaid lifted her hair, wiped the bar beneath it, and let it fall back. There was a quiet about the room—a soft moment as though the whole room was taking a breath in unison. Then the fake leather door opened and three thick men entered, paused looking around them, and moved toward the bar. One of them, wearing a sheer yellow nylon shirt with the tail out, grabbed one of the habitués, who was at least twenty years older than he was, and began dancing with her. When the band switched to "The Tennessee Waltz" he and the woman were still two-stepping. A truck driver with his left arm in a sling was dancing with a skinny blonde and holding her with the hand of his good arm on her bottom.

"Let's dance," Fletcher said.

He put his arm around Sunny and squeezed her to him as they walked to the dance floor. They waltzed a few minutes. By now the man in the yellow nylon shirt was largely supporting his partner whose head floundered on his shoulder.

"I got a son," Sunny heard the woman mutter to him, "he give me nothing but trouble all his life," she said. She had

15

dark pouches like brown pudding under each eye and a long dangling rhinestone earring hung onto the shoulder of the man's nylon shirt like an epaulette.

The music stopped and they stood with their arms around each other until it started again, this time with a polka. Fletcher stomped his right foot twice as he'd seen it done in Pfluggerville, Texas, and they were joined by the truck driver and the blonde, the sagging couple, and Alma the go-go dancer with one of the marines. The marine gave a rebel yell and began whirling Alma in her glasses and torn hose, pumping her arm vigorously. The marine and Alma, Fletcher and Sunny, competed and gradually the other two couples retired. The band played faster and faster while a few spectators clapped and Floyd, the proprietress, whose real name was Claudine, smiled from behind the bar. Fletcher whirled Sunny around the floor until she was out of breath and helpless with laughter. When the music stopped Fletcher and the marine slapped each other on the back in mutual admiration.

"But we were best," Sunny whispered, kissing Fletcher on the side of the face. "You're devastating," she said to him going back to the booth.

"The polka is one of my specialties," he admitted, "but if you liked that, just follow me, lady," he said.

They finished their beers and closed the doors on a wailing "Cold, Cold Heart."

Sunny and Fletcher held hands, swinging their arms, and Fletcher sang a rearranged Woody Guthrie.

Ain't it a shame to love Sunny on Sunday, ain't it a shame . . .
Ain't it a shame to love Sunny on Sunday, ain't it a shame . . .
Ain't it a shame to love Sunny on Sunday,

16

When you got Monday, Tuesday, Wednesday . . .
O-o-oh—Friday, Saturday, ain't it a shame. . . .

It was three blocks to his apartment. They walked down a line of scaly sycamores, clipped and doctored, tall and regal, the light night sparkling against their white scaly trunks. A street washer sprayed the street, barreling down the road like some huge animal, leaving a wide glittery swath behind it. From a convertible stopped for a light, music wafted over the street, and two women sat on a stoop, their cigarettes glowing intermittently like fireflies. Fletcher sang on, occasionally adding his country yodel.

He was still singing when they rounded the corner and saw the cruiser stopped. The red and white lights circled in silence atop the car, their rays sweeping the newly opened windows of the old houses, beckoning, so that soon a crowd gathered at the corner under the streetlight to stare nervously up and down the dark street. From the cruiser spouts of radio bulletins ripped obscenely through the peaceful night.

"That's the way it is, isn't it?" Sunny said later. "Before something awful happens you're most off your guard. It was such a peaceful night. You know what I mean, Fletcher, maybe that's why it happened. The moon was full. I remember I looked up and it seemed to be sitting on a tree limb. It's true, Fletcher, people more often go mad at a full moon. Old things are true, it's the new things that are lies."

They joined a group of people beneath the streetlight—an old man, a young couple, an effeminate young man with a poodle. Porch lights flashed on, families hung from upstairs windows watching.

"What happened?" Fletcher asked the fellow with the poodle.

The man hesitated a moment not sure he was being addressed and then turned a blond ageless face toward Fletcher.

17

"Chasing some man is all I know," he said, shifting the dog leash nervously. He patted the head of the big brown poodle that sat looking up the street along with the people. "I was just walking my dog when I saw the excitement. Always some poor bastard being chased around here."

They were all quiet a moment and the radio blurted out some unidentifiable words and an address.

The old man who stood with his back to them turned and stared at them a minute. "They run him up the block and into the alley," he volunteered. His cracked hand trembled under the streetlight as he pointed toward the alley entrance in the middle of the block.

It was a narrow street of two- and three-story Victorian row houses, each with a narrow yard in front enclosed by a black wrought-iron fence, alike as a row of shoe boxes. It was a neat, clean street, whose old homes had been, for the most part, remodeled and their windows grilled. The neighborhood had been part of the black ghetto until in recent years realtors and civil servants, seeing the sturdy old houses convenient to the Capitol, began pushing the black people out, remodeling their houses, and barring their windows.

There were police cars now at either end of the block, and more and more people were gathering on each of the corners under the streetlights. A big car passed at the intersection and slowed to watch the activity.

A plainclothesman, a clatter of keys hanging from his belt, strode toward them. He had a clean scrubbed look and a starched shirt with fresh laundry folds. "Anybody see a colored man run by here a few minutes ago?" he asked. He spoke with a businessman's Virginia accent as he looked over the group, finally settling his question on Fletcher. Behind him like a consort, stood a patrolman in motorcycle uniform with small squinting eyes and broad flat hips like a country girl.

Fletcher shook his head.

"You people better be careful—this man we're looking for is armed." He waited for his words to sink in and seeing no response he moved away, followed by the patrolman in his tight black boots.

Once they were gone the old man whispered in his broken voice, "I seen him. He went up the alley." The old man looked down the street and despite his wispy white hair and the deeply weathered face, creased and gnarled, of one who'd spent his life outdoors, his profile was finely etched like a child's. "Ran right up this sidewalk and into that alley," he said. "But they got it blocked off. He can't get out," he said, peering into the group of spectators to see who might be listening to him. His eyes caught Sunny's and held them a moment until she looked away toward the sycamore in front of them sprinkled with buttonballs. They reminded her of gumdrop trees she had made at Christmas. Year after year, blue, pink, multicolored gumdrop trees.

Like conspirators they all peered into the cloaked darkness toward the alley where the old man had pointed, and a potential of violence grew around them. The flashing lights, the radio, the gathering police, and the very presence of those impassive faces, their calmly restrained, tense movements like actors', their clean dark clothes, antiseptic as dyed supermarket fruit, all provoked fear and guilt and memories of violence until they each stood with the whole of their experience of violence wrapped around them, contained there, charging the air.

Sunny shivered.

"Cat crossed your grave," the old man whispered to her, and then as though he'd read her thoughts, "We could all be killed," he muttered. And when no one responded, "We could all be killed right here on this corner." He looked down at the concrete walk beneath his feet as though he could feel his head against it. "Chasing him like an animal," he muttered. "A nice-looking young man," he said. "Chasing him up the street Lincoln lived on."

Sunny turned and looked into his faded eyes.

"He had mistresses up and down this street. Had a colored woman and a white woman and an Indian woman and a Chinese woman lived right up there where that laundry is at. He weren't no racist, Abraham Lincoln. That's a lie started by them CIA men." A side of his face fluttered. "Chased him right up this street, blood running down him. See the blood?" He pointed up the sidewalk before them. There was nothing but shadowed limbs.

A breeze pushed across Sunny's cheeks. Her eyes ached from staring at the alley and she turned away a moment looking up at the sky through the bare limbs of the tree. When she turned back, her eyes stopped at the old red-brick house next to the alley. It had a front porch with brick pillars and a trellis between them. The house itself, like three or four others in the block, was completely dark, oblivious to the activity. It was a nice house, she thought. Had it been hers she'd have hung a swing on the porch and been sitting there this evening. She had grown up in a house with a front porch swing. She had spent long hours with hardly a consciousness of time rocking in the swing, staring at the night, singing, daydreaming peacefully. But now it would be different. Now probably she would be afraid at night on a porch alone.

She leaned against Fletcher's arm, closing her eyes, pitying the man being chased, thinking how afraid he must be. She could hear the old man's wheezed breathing beside her. When she looked up Fletcher seemed unaware of her, absorbed with the scene like a man looking through peepholes in fences at building-sites, peering at holes in the ground, at men moving the earth around. She released his arm and looked back toward the alley in the middle of the block.

Even before she heard the old man she saw the movement on the porch behind the trellis. It was slight as though someone had slowly turned his head. She strained staring at the spot and wondering what led her to see a nearly imperceptible movement.

"There he is," the old man whispered beside her. "There he is!" The old man's hands waved excitedly. "I got eyes like a hawk," he said. "And I can smell like a shark. A shark can smell blood for miles. I can smell people. Every person on this earth has a different smell," he whispered. "I can smell death. I got gypsy blood in me."

The figure moved. She saw his crouched body cautiously edge down the porch toward the stairs. Underneath them was an opening which led beneath the porch. Sunny stepped back with her hands crossed over her mouth wishing she'd not seen him. She heard the police car start and watched it roll up in front of the house. The thick patrolman in the motorcycle boots knelt behind a metal chair in the next yard. He pulled his gun out of his holster and pointed it toward the porch, resting it on the side of the chair. Suddenly a spotlight from the car flashed on, sweeping the house till it struck. The figure was trapped, caught in the light and for an instant he hesitated looking either way.

"Okay, throw out your gun," the policeman called.

On the porch the gun glistened in the man's hand and the shot was a sudden high brassy pop. There was a cry from the people on the corner, who scattered, ducking behind cars and trees, and running away down the street.

Cursing, Fletcher pulled Sunny behind a car, and the old man followed them, kneeling close to Sunny, clutching her arm. His hands were shaking.

After the shot the man ran, jumping a fence and then another until his feet hit the sidewalk with a thud. He ran counter to the police car with three policemen behind him, running toward the intersection away from Sunny and Fletcher, running in that frantic, ultimate way a man runs when there is everything at stake, toward the intersection that marked the beginning of the ghetto where the streets were suddenly darker.

"They'll lose him over there, unless they head him off," Fletcher said.

"They gonna shoot him," the old man muttered.

There was no sound but running and the people moving out again until suddenly there was a plane overhead drowning out everything else. Sunny watched as the policeman with the wide hips stopped and raised his arm. Over the sound of the plane she heard the reports.

Like a flawed film the movement of the running man altered, his body caught, stopped, suspended against the roaring dark. He took a few ragged strides and fell forward on his face, his feet rocking up behind him. The sound of the plane died away and it was quiet on the street except for a car a distance away. Cautiously, the police were walking toward the body crumpled on the street.

"My God," Sunny said again and again. She heard herself but seemed unable to stop. She felt Fletcher's arm around her waist and he turned toward her, but she pulled away and started walking down the block across the intersection toward the man's body.

A policeman bent over him and lifted a silver revolver. It shone under the dim streetlight, delicate and lovely, like a wounded bird, the barrel down as the policeman rose wearily and carried it to the prowl car where another man was talking on the radio. There were more police cars now. The plainclothesman with the keys watched absently as Sunny and Fletcher and the others passed and gathered around the man's body. They stood in a half circle, quietly, feeling irrelevant, like intruders.

The man lay on his stomach, his arms under him, his face averted. He was neatly dressed, his pants creased. A rhinestone sparkled from each cuff link. Sunny studied the back of his neck, his square fingernails, the slender line of his body, expecting somehow to recognize something about him. "Is he dead?" she asked barely audibly and no one answered.

Is he dead? Is he dead? Is he dead? Is he dead? Her mind echoed.

There were others now, black people joining them, leaving their stoops, emerging from the laundromat down the block. An enormous black woman pushed through the crowd and peered over the shoulders of the old man who pointed at the body. "Lord amercy," she said.

"His feet are pointing at us," the old man said.

The man wore high-cut buckled Italian-style shoes and one leg lay twisted so that his feet were both turned toward them awkwardly.

"It's a sign he's gonna haunt us," the old man said.

"That's sure a sign," the big black woman added.

"He's gonna haunt us . . . and God's gonna punish you," the old man shrieked toward the policeman kneeling beside the body.

They were talking now, the people on the street, commenting among themselves.

"What'd he do?" Fletcher asked.

The policeman stood up and began writing in a notebook. He waited awhile before answering.

"Armed robbery," he said without looking up.

The spectators looked again at the man sprawled on the street as though that added information might help them understand the body lying there. Sunny imagined the man entering a store, pulling the silver pistol from his pocket. . . .

The priest appeared from nowhere, parting the group and pushing past Sunny, a short, ruddy-skinned thick man with a dirty collar and curly unkempt black hair that fell in his face when he knelt beside the body. There was something about the man that made the group more uncomfortable—something about the scruffiness of his dress, the intensity of his movements, the great jagged concern on his face like a wound. He appeared as though he'd been waiting, hiding in the alley watching, knowing it would happen.

"Is he dead?" he asked the policeman. His voice was low and professional but flat.

The policeman spoke quietly to the priest who then bent over the man and began praying into his ear.

"May our Lord Jesus Christ absolve you, and I by His authority absolve you of your sins . . . in the name of the Father and of the Son and of the Holy Ghost."

He pulled himself up and made the sign of the cross over the man. Then he bent back, still on his knees, and began to pray again quietly. A drop of sweat fell from the priest's face onto the man's coat while behind them a siren grew closer.

"Our Father, the great leveler who knows the ways of the alleys and streets and dark paths some of us are driven through, please know that I love you and give you my soul in peace. In the name of the Father and of the Son and of the Holy Ghost. Amen."

The priest stood up wearily and gave the knees of his pants a half-hearted brush with the back of his hand. He turned to the spectators and seemed about to speak regarding the man lying there, but the ambulance rounded the corner, its siren dying, and they turned their attention away from him.

"Timothy Rose is a black buzzard pervert," the old man muttered beside Sunny. "A buzzard, flying around in the alleys. . . ."

The red light flashed over them as they turned the body. Sunny looked away and saw a boy standing at the edge of the crowd. He was a child, an uncommonly thin black boy with big oval eyes and prominent ears, and pants that were too big so that they were gathered around the waist until they resembled a long skirt. In his hands was a sheaf of handbills. He gazed with the calm acceptance children have for the bizarre and cruel as the ambulance men opened the doors and slid the stretcher into the ambulance like a loaf of bread and slammed the doors afterward. The ambulance cruised to the end of the block before it turned on the siren and picked up speed, and only then did people begin to disperse. When the boy passed her, Sunny picked up one of the handbills that had slipped from his hands.

MOTHER MYRA, SPIRITUAL HEALER AND ADVISOR, the handbill read.

The priest stood staring down at the dark stain on the street. Sunny saw him quickly bend down, run his fingers through the uneven pool, and cross himself. He turned to leave but brushing Sunny's arm he stopped a moment.

"I apologize," he said standing very close to her.

The streetlight fell across the side of his face. He did not meet her eyes but averted his permitting her to gaze at him as an object without challenge or defense. He stood, his face damp, his mouth thick, either cheek indented with scars, and like a caste mark the touch of blood stood on his forehead. Sunny felt herself recoil and she stepped away from him. His eyes moved to hers apologetically, then he passed and disappeared down the dark, bare street.

I am making a list of the obscene. His death was obscene. Lying in the street, his body perfect, complete, whole except for the holes made by the bullets. There was no dignity. His body writhed. Whoever was on the street or leaning from a window could see. His feet jerked. I wanted to turn the tail of his jacket down so it would be neat.

There was no privacy. They went through his pockets. It was obscene.

Do men get used to it? Do men get used to it in war, someone dying in the open like that? Fletcher says no. But he doesn't know. He says that to have an answer. He's not been to war. But he could go. He fights on weekends drinking beer and two weeks in the summers. He hates it.

You are too upset, he said. Don't be so upset.

How can you just accept it as something that happens, I asked.

Because it just happens.

You accept too much, I accuse him.

He thinks women can afford to be emotional and self-righteous because it doesn't matter. A man, he says, has to pay for his differences. He hates the war but he would go. I'm not the first American pragmatist, he says. I don't want to go to prison. You'd kill people and call that pragmatic, I said. He is quiet. He doesn't like to talk like that. He doesn't like to disagree and on serious matters we always disagree, and I get upset, and he hates it. Good-time Charlie and Charlene, that's us. He takes it all calmly. The Congress, the war, the killing, all the rotten dirtiness of it. Writing my father's lies for him. He absorbs it. If you lived with it all your life, I say. . . . That makes him mad.

But dying like that on the street built for cars to drive over. Men have spit there where he lay on the street. . . . And I worry about his lying in an unholy place when someone has just put a hole in him and he probably lived in unholy places all his life.

And here she is, Miss Sunny Tidwell interviewing the recent dead: Was there anything holy about your life, young man?

Screw you, he, in his white robes, replies.

Yes, you're absolutely right, Miss Tidwell says. What right

have I to ask? What did I do? I didn't grab the cop's arm. I didn't cry out. But do you mind if I wonder about you? Will it matter? Will it make any difference to anyone, anywhere, even to myself?

I feel very close to you, you see. We stood waiting and I felt your fear, your panic. I saw your last moment, your body's external response to the bullet. In one of those moments as I watched, you ceased to live. How? Did your heart stop first, did you stop breathing? Shouldn't there have been some manifestation, shouldn't we have felt the moment, known when life stopped?

When you lay grotesquely on the street I wanted to cover your body, shield your body with my own, give you some of my life, lie on the street, wallow there beside you and scream. Only the priest tried something.

He turns away. The back of his robe is black. I am lying.

It is important that I am honest about my role. He was a stranger. To me my reaction to his death was more important than his death. I do not know how his hand or his body or his mouth felt. To me he was a tragic incident. What was it to how many others? Was he married? Was he in love? Was he writing a poem, paying out a suit? Did he have a child, a pregnant wife, a sick mother? Did he have friends who will miss him terribly?

What equals that death? Another death? Had he killed? Does death equal death? Is there an equation that can be worked out? Can we measure his mother's love, the number of his children and their needs? How much did it hurt? Did he feel a terrible pain? Just what should be my appropriate response?

It is important that I remember my place. I am an onlooker. I never touched him. It is unfair for me to sympathize too much, for I cannot . . . really.

Some people choose it, dying in public like that. Pouring

gasoline over themselves. There could be something good about it maybe. The ultimate obscenity—reminding people of death. Look, I'm dying like you're going to! The ultimate personal obscenity in the face of the ultimate obscenity. What is it? Death? Death to death? The joke's on you, young man, burning there. Or is it letting that man die there on the street, shooting that man on the first warm day of spring?

My mother didn't mind the idea of dying in public. You see, he is the second person I've seen die. His body was perfect. My mother was shattered in a car. She had been wanting to die for a long time, long before she entered the car that day. She'd mentioned it occasionally. She had begun dying long ago when some moment she succumbed to the idea without fear, preparing herself, looking foward to its being over like a doctor's appointment. She had already separated herself, withdrawn from her husband and her daughter. We lived separate lives, passing one another. Passing one another in halls, wearing our thin sheets of scar tissue over our unhealed wounds, the two opposite charges and their unstable offspring. And over it all was the sound of my father—always loud and effusive, slamming car doors, shouting through doorways, into phones, his manner always pressing.

I think how she must have felt driving toward the underpass. I wonder if she planned it ahead. Did she suddenly see the stout concrete walls, dense, strong like my father's name, and smile as she pulled the steering wheel to the right. Or maybe it was a mistake, a dizzy moment and the horror of its suddenly looming before her.

Did she feel the impact which left her body crushed, alive but only for several hours? Did she in any second regret it? Did she think at all? Were her eyes closed? Did she see her blood drip into the ashtray?

I remember her white body breathing its last breath in the

hospital room. Her breathing stopped gently like an hour-glass.

Like the death of an old, old woman.

I wanted her to regain consciousness so I could shriek, Look at me, Mother; remember me, Mother, don't die! It was purely selfish. Her death was a denying of my significance. To whom do we matter if it isn't our parents? I knew that by then. There are so few who ever care if we have nightmares in the night. Isn't that why our God knew the number of hairs on our heads? Her death was a dwindling of my substance that I cannot recover.

She died and I have subdivided. Now there are the parts of me and another, all without benefit of matrimony. And it was easy, thank you. I would like a girl. It is a totally selfish wish. I want a little me so I can go through it all again and watch and shout directions. I will rest and watch. I will lie on a bed like a queen with a hat on and direct. It will be fun. She will be company. Someone to sing to. Someone to bring my cigarettes and hold in my lap and talk to.

I will name her Eleanor because I wanted to be named Eleanor. It is neutral. She can be sad and not feel guilty. My name is not neutral. It is a contradiction. "Tidwell" a heavy dull word evoking the rectangular density of a barn; an ugly sturdy word like the Tidwell relatives who send away for their oversized shoes.

Cap, you'd never be elected if it weren't for your legion of thick-legged relatives. Oh, Mama, Mama, Mama.

They chose Sunny. The hopeful optimism of aging parents expecting more than possible. Twelve years of war and a child. "Sunny," the rainbow child—six healthy pounds of barter and referee.

My grandmother dreamed my name. Waking my grand-father in the middle of the night, she announced, Leita and

Cap's child will be named "Sunny." I saw it on one of Cap's posters in Coca-Cola red letters.

That night I was born. My grandfather claimed it was "Sonny" she dreamed. They argued about it until he died of a heart attack one cold February afternoon. Everyone else in the family believed her. My mother's family believed in such things. Fundamentalist religion, fortune-tellers, ouija boards, talking tables, spirits, chiropractors, and individuals gifted to remove warts. Every major event in their lives had been predicted by one type of seer or another. My name was a supernatural incident in a long line of supernatural incidents.

Eleanor Worthington. I wanted to be named Eleanor Worthington. "Eleanor": poised, self-contained, serene, above the battle. "Worthington": absolutely safe. We lived beside Worthingtons. Our houses were separated by a brick wall and a tall hedge and a lot of money and dignity. They were very rich and very clean. Their house sat on a winter-green lawn, each tiny blade perfect, fragile, soft enough to be stroked. There were no flowers. No smelly marigolds. I planted marigolds every year. Their heads grew too heavy, bending the stalks. The blossoms faced the ground.

Each evening in the summer the Worthingtons sat on their green lawn in their white painted lawn chairs, and a black servant in a crisp, white jacket rolled out a white tea cart. They drank from tall frosted glasses. Like a movie scene in Connecticut, I thought. Two beautiful old people with white hair sitting beside the white tea cart under the shade of their very own tall oak trees. On Sundays the servant drove them in their big black car. Their oak trees were taller than everyone else's.

On late summer nights I would climb on top of the brick fence and peek through the hedge into their living room. There was dark woodwork and a huge mirror on the wall. My

the first of the political explanations that to him explained all of life.

I never wore my hair like that again. I hated them. I wouldn't pass the house when they were out-of-doors. They had committed the unforgivable. They had not liked me. That was failure . . . utter failure. It was our ethic. To be unpopular meant there was something wrong, a flaw within, a secret sin. Through school we were tested. Contests. Elections. Preachers and mothers said good girls were popular.

I daydreamed revenge. The Worthingtons, struck by guilt, would send me gifts. A white eyelet evening gown with black velvet ribbons. They would wave at me through the windows. They would telephone. And finally one night the servant would appear at our door. It would be snowing and he would beg to see me. They are dying, he'd say, and they are pleading for you. And I (in a cloak) would follow him to their bedroom where they would be lying side by side on satin pillows in their large Victorian canopied bed.

You are a lovely, sweet child, they'd say, please forgive us.

I waited three years; until we moved away. But they never waved out the window or telephoned and the servant never came and the winter grass was always neat and green. And I don't know when they died. Even their house is gone now. Torn down and the winter green is paved over, and I'll never know if they were sad people or whether they might have had a little girl named Eleanor.

But maybe I know as much about the Worthingtons as anyone else I know. Maybe whatever we know about people is just what we daydream, even what we know about ourselves. I know less about myself. I have a mental block. Maybe that's why I'm drifting along.

For god's sake, do something, my father says.

But I meet such nice people at the unemployment office, Daddy dear. Besides I screw a lot.

33

One female child who's a bum! Who won't hold a job, won't even get married and procreate so I might have decent grandchildren!

But there are many things to do and many things to see, and many miles before we sleep, Daddy dear, see here, see here.

II

Sunny. Sitting on a red leatherette stool at a drug counter drinking lukewarm, bitter coffee. With her spoon she tries separating the tiny bubbles of oil floating on top until a grilled cheese sandwich borne on a pink plastic plate appears before her. The middle-aged waitress with rouged, wrinkled cheeks and "Kate" stitched on her green nylon uniform begins refilling red plastic catsup containers, wiping the lids on a ragged white towel. Outside the plate glass window, past a poster proclaiming a fast, safe sleep potion, there is no sun, only grayness and a chilly damp wind. Across the street a buzzsaw drones where men are shaving the limbs from a big sycamore. Small branches, snapped off and caught by the wind, glide down like torn kites, to be raked together and loaded into a truck.

The drugstore was a cluttered neighborhood affair without chain affiliation. The druggist supplemented his income by taking numbers for his brother-in-law, a small mustachioed man who wore a Sherlock Holmes hat and fronted as a cabbie. Two legitimate cabbies hung out there so that the neighborhood ladies had the convenience of either getting a cab or playing a number at their leisure. One of the cabbies, a white man who wore wraparound sunshades was arguing over a story in the *Afro-American* about a black rock-and-roll singer arrested for the statutory rape of three white teenage girls. The charge had been changed to contributing to the delinquency of a minor, but the cabbie claimed he should have been charged with rape and the girls beaten twice a day till they were old enough to be charged with prostitution. He read the *Afro-American* every day so that he could argue with the black pharmacist who was presently questioning how this short, skinny rock-and-roll singer could have raped three healthy teenage girls—and after a performance. The cabbie suggested he was a judo expert, and the second cabbie, a former hospital orderly who read the daily doctor's column in the newspaper, pointed out that some people's metabolism is strongest late at night.

Next to Sunny sat a small woman wearing a net scarf over her brown and gray permanent-curls. She wore a printed cotton dress with a dark wool suit coat over it and looked as dry as the liverwurst sandwich she was eating.

"I'm so nervous I can hardly eat," she confided to Sunny. She looked to Kate to include her in the conversation. "I've just been to the morgue to identify my husband's body."

"Jesus, that's awful," Kate said.

"He's been dead since the first of the month and they never called me till yesterday," the woman said. She paused to pull a paper napkin from the metal container between them and blot her small mouth. "He had my name and his VA papers in his pocket. I can't understand why they didn't get in touch with me sooner. . . . It was terrible," she said, shaking her head. "I just could barely tell him by his features. I thought I was gonna faint. Just last week I had to take a bus to Baltimore and I didn't know then if I'd make it."

Kate turned and began dipping glasses into a sudsless gray water and stacking them on a tray.

"He looked so awful I just could barely tell him by his features," the woman repeated. "They said he died of sclerosis of the liver and yellow jaundice, but really he just drank himself to death." She sipped her coke.

"That's a shame," Sunny said.

"Yeah, and he was a right nice-looking little man when I married him. I haven't lived with him since fifty-eight cause he took to drinking so bad I just couldn't take it."

Kate moved off to refill the coffee cup of one of the cab drivers and the woman took a dainty bite of her liverwurst sandwich and chewed slowly.

Over the rim of her coffee cup Sunny looked outside where a black figure stared up at the emasculated tree. He stood with his hands at his sides, upright and straight like some inappropriate black vertical smear in a sea of shifting gray horizontals.

A blackbird, Sunny thought. Coarse and sad and out of place.

He held his head cocked to one side as though listening for some inner groan from the tree. He seemed curiously immobile amid the working men who moved around him as though he didn't exist. When he spoke they stopped, surprised, and one began shaking his hand and gesturing toward the tree. The priest clasped his hands behind his back and nodded, and the man made a last sweeping gesture and returned to raking the small broken limbs.

The priest walked to the corner looking down the street for a bus but instead of waiting he crossed the street against the light toward the drugstore.

"You know," the little woman said to Sunny, "I had a

premonition. My ears rang for a week. Even my landlady said her ears had been ringing, and then soon as I heard the news he was dead they stopped ringing, and my landlady said hers stopped around then, too."

The priest appeared in the doorway.

"It was sure a premonition," the woman said. "Do you believe in premonitions?" the woman asked Sunny.

"Oh, yes, I believe in premonitions," Sunny said. "Don't you have any children to help you?"

"I have a son, but not by this man," the woman said, grateful for Sunny's question. "He's my second husband. But my son hated this man. He used to get drunk and knock me around. My son liked to killed him one time."

Sunny shivered as the priest passed behind them and took a seat at an angle across from them.

"Cat crossed your grave," the woman said to her.

His collar was dirty and his hands shook as he lighted a cigarette. He was not old, maybe not forty, but he looked weary and beaten like someone whose life was a series of misfortunes.

"What'll it be, Father?" Kate asked.

Outside the saw ceased and the men were breaking for lunch, some of them sitting where the sycamore limbs had shaded.

"I just been telling these ladies, Father, that I just come from the morgue. I had to identify my husband's body."

"God care for you," he said quietly, not looking at the woman. His voice had a resonance that carried so that the cabbies glanced down the counter at the priest.

The woman was embarrassed. "Well, Father, I wasn't with him at the end. We were separated—he drank a lot—and they just notified me. He died of sclerosis of the liver and yellow jaundice. Drank himself to death. . . . I tell you, Father, it takes a saint to live with a drinking man."

Sunny felt the priest looking at her and automatically turned toward the woman.

"Now he's gonna have a proper burial. I signed all the papers today. My sister said, maybe I oughta just give him to research cause I know I done the best I could to get him buried, but I said, no, I just can't do that to family . . . not to family."

Kate leaned against the back of the ice cream bins and began scraping under her fingernails with the cuptowel wrapped around her waist. "There's been two times in my life," she said, "when somebody called and said relatives had died. Once somebody phoned and said my mother died, and I went all the way home to West Virginia and she weren't no more dead than a jackrabbit. Then somebody phoned and said my son, who was in Vietnam, was dead. I liked to died. But he's fat and sassy as ever. He'll be getting out in October."

They were quiet a moment. The cab drivers were laughing and a fat fly crawled up the window behind Kate.

"Yes, I said to my sister, I can't give his body to medical research, not family. Now he's gonna have a proper burial Monday. I tried to get him into Arlington but they were full up. Maybe you'd like to come, Father," she said.

The priest's hand wavered on his cup and coffee splashed onto the saucer.

Kate reached for the cup, filled it again and emptied the saucer.

"I'm grateful," the priest said quietly. He looked at none of them but spread his hands before him on the counter. They were short and stubby and the black hairs on his knuckles were coarse and curly. Sunny imagined a man would stare in a mirror at his deformity in the same manner.

They were all watching him uneasily, the widow chewing the last bite of the liverwurst sandwich, waiting, expecting some bizarre disclosure, but he remained quiet. From the other end of the counter one of the cabbies called to Kate and she left, walking heavily in her white wedge waitress shoes.

Sunny, not wanting to be left alone with the priest, and seeing the widow dab at her mouth and reach for her cracked plastic handbag, hurriedly pulled her money from her pocket. She stacked her change next to the pink plastic plate and wished the woman luck and left quickly, not looking again at the priest but waving to Kate who was too busy now talking to the cabbies to notice.

Mystery Sniper in Southeast, Sunny read on her way out, glancing at a newspaper.

No papers for me, thank you. All my life he sat at the table bellowing over the news, talking to himself, addressing the news to us but really talking to himself, gulping coffee, us sitting silently, letting him go on, hating him. . . .

A daily following of the world? Too gruesome. What exists in my world is what I see. People on stools in drugstores, leaning out windows, calling children home. What happens to most people I see every day? The detached happenings men use to thread the tales of history . . . I can do without. I will live with those people I see. All those unseen, mythical places, people with custom-tailored clothes who make history . . . let them have it. Always the news blurting, thrust upon me. Now I can reject it. All those people playing games with other people's lives . . .

Outside it was winter again and she pulled her collar up, trying to shield her ears from the wind, and began walking toward town. She was in the middle of the block when she heard his footsteps behind her. She walked more slowly, self-conscious of her walk and her body. The footsteps adjusted, staying behind her. She put her hands in her pocket and refused to look back. After a while she stopped at a small park and sat on a bench, waiting for him to join her.

"You're from the CIA," she said when he sat beside her. "I recognize you by your green hat." She turned to look at him, and while he wore no hat his eyes were clearer now and very green. In the vivid daylight she saw again that his cheeks were deeply pitted and scarred. She smiled and looked across the road where two policemen chatted beside their dogs.

"You're very astute," he said. "I am a spy—for myself though. I'm naturally curious."

And also lonely, Sunny thought. "Why are you spying on me?"

"It's divine providence. I've seen you two times within a short while and I'd never seen you before . . . and I thought of you."

"Vibrations?"

"Something like that."

"Did you know the man?"

He turned away, glancing at the next bench where a wino slept, a newspaper tenting his head.

"No . . . he was just a man. I've seen men die on the streets before."

"There's something particularly awful about someone dying on a street. It made me think of a public execution. I wondered what he might have thought lying there, knowing it might be his last thought."

"It was probably no worse than a man's last thought anywhere," the priest said.

"But think how frightening it must be with a strange crowd around you, watching."

"Once I was with a man dying in the street and a motorist came along—a big white man—and he pulled to a halt right in front of the man, and honked. . . ." His voice sounded gray like the day and she became aware of the cars honking on the avenue.

She looked down at his scuffed orange-brown shoes. He seemed very strong and composed when he spoke but in repose he was sad and disarranged.

He thinks I need him. He thinks he'll help me. Startled, she looked away, thinking she had read his mind.

The city air was heavy and abrasive. She felt she might catch it in her hand and feel the grit.

"I don't think I've ever talked to a priest before," she said.

He shifted on the bench turning toward her. "You'll find me like most men," he said . . . "perhaps a bit more haunted."

And as if to prove it, he took her hand and ran his fingers along the bones of each of her fingers. His hands were firm and unhesitant. He released her hand smiling and they rose and followed the old brick walks toward town, past the newly-green tended lawns of the Capitol, past lines of chartered buses, and old drivers waiting wearily in their seats. They walked easily beside each other, feeling no necessity to speak.

"Do you know the old grotto?" she asked him.

She led him down the hill to the small cave in front of the Capitol half hidden by trees and shrubs, an oasis of mystery with an iron gate. Inside it was damp and private.

"Let me tell you about this grotto and Saint Washington," Sunny whispered. "Once upon a time Saint Washington appeared here to the Indians and said 'Upon this hill I will build a country of just men, reincarnated spirits of the great Christians.' And the Indians, having heard of the goodness of the early Christians and the teachings of Jesus from a kind old Viking missionary, wept with joy and said, 'Thank you, Saint Washington, we will build a city here and name it Washington, and a great nation will come forth and bring peace and bounty and scientific inventions.' And the Indians set about erecting a great Indian city.

"One day men with light-colored skin appeared, and the

Indians, thinking they were the promised Christians, yelped with joy and ran toward them bearing gifts of intricate and beautiful handiwork. And the light-colored men, afraid of anyone unlike themselves, raised their salt-water-rusted rifles and shot them. And this is all that remains of the Indian city."

"That's a very sad story," he said. He smiled at her with his green eyes and in the shadows, his ravaged face mostly hidden, he was not completely unattractive. What a queer, attentive man, she thought.

They heard laughter and children approaching so they left, crossing the street to the dreary fountains where the statue of Columbus stared in the background. Sunny skipped along the side of the fountain, teetering on the edge beside the children, They crossed the torn streets, the littered pawn shops, and the dirty windows of bondsmen. They looked at the outside stalls of cheap bookstores and rummaged the stacks inside. They stood before a window of wigs, strung from a clothesline, propped on boxes, adorning plasticene skulls—blonde, red, black, striped, carrot, gray-blue hair, eighty-nine, sixty-nine, thirty-nine dollar wigs, falls, and wiglets. They all circled one long blonde hair fall, flowing past the shoulders of a plastic bust, bare from bosom to head except for the pasted-on real hair eyelashes sprinkled with rhinestones, shading large azure-blue painted eyes.

"Are you really a priest?" Sunny asked him a little hesitantly over coffee in a doughnut shop.

"Father Timothy Rose, excommunicate," he said bowing his head and stirring his coffee. "But I am a priest of the city, my apostolate, to the misbegotten. Bums, you could call them. I minister to crumbling buildings, rusting file cabinets, blackened buses, clogged gutters, and the bodies that lie therein." He smiled at himself caustically in the mirror behind the counter opposite them. "Seldom are the bodies more

43

alive than the other objects. I serve as mediator, flagellant, mnemonic conscience, burier, and object of curiosity among the no longer curious. I observe and wince, wondering when I will go either blind or dead as they. It is amazing that the rusty needles and empty pockets and the cold and the indignities of their lives have not immunized them. The most drunken staggering bum crawling along the street still cries and hurts when kicked. Furthermore," he said, cutting into a chocolate doughnut, "he has enemies and lovers. Alcohol is not the great anesthetizer it is said to be."

He sipped coffee, watching himself in the mirror again and then turning to her as if for a minute he'd forgotten her. . . . "But to answer your question, I am no longer recognized by the Roman Church. I am what they call 'irregular.' That's the term for men who've married or run away or gone mad. I've done all of them. I'm married to these streets."

One of the waitresses, a young black girl wearing wooden African earrings, had been listening to him in awe, and when he met her gaze she turned away and laughed uncomfortably. He looked at her sadly.

Later they sat on the steps of a post office and listened to a blind woman on the corner swat the strings of her old guitar. There was a tin cup attached to the head of her guitar and her wide black face was unsmiling as she sang . . .

> Got a home in that rock, can't you see . . .
> Got a home in that rock, can't you see . . .

Shoppers passed in gusts, like wind, and now and then coins plunked dully into her tin cup. Between songs she shifted on her canvas stool and emptied a coin or two into the pocket of the long cotton apron she wore under her coat. Then she'd start again, her body rocking gently as she sang.

Sunny and Timothy Rose listened, sitting on the grimy steps watching the knots of people waiting for the buses that swooshed past pouring their vile exhalations into the faces of waiting passengers.

"This is an ugly-people day," Sunny said. "Have you noticed people look ugly today?"

"People look like what's around them," he said.

"Yes, I guess that's true. It's really always the same problem watching people," Sunny said. "There are so many different faces, but there are so few words to label them with. Happiness, sadness. I guess it's just the words that are limited, and we have to force our feelings into them. Everyone should have his own words. That's the only way it would ever be accurate."

The gray day darkened early and the lights of the buildings came on and the old woman still sang.

I got a mansion waiting for me . . .
Angel, prepare my mansion, I'm coming home. . . .

They sat together comfortably watching the day end and the night grow. The street began to clog with homebound traffic. The buses grew more crowded and stuffed and the people rushed more and more. Ladies in hats flagged cabs and a young mother hurriedly pushed a sleeping child. Students stood in little groups, holding their books, and laughing. Black ladies, domestic workers carrying shoe totes, changed buses wearily. Three young toughs stood back from the bus stop watching the women's purses, waiting for a careless arm.

A clock several blocks away began to strike five o'clock.

Each burden he'll bear, each sorrow and care . . .

the old woman sang . . .

On the Jericho Road, there's room for just two. . . .

Suddenly from an office building several stories above the ground a man's voice was heard. It was strong and resonant,

45

joining the old woman's, smoothing the twanging sound of the guitar, modulating the old broken voice, raising the dimension of sound. It lifted the faces of the young toughs, of the bus patrons, of Sunny, and the priest, and all those around.

Fletcher phoned from the office. He let it ring six times then hung up and tried again, hoping he'd dialed the wrong number. He wanted Sunny to meet him at Floyd's but then of course she would be wandering. When she was upset she wandered and might not come home at all that night. If she had the car she might drive to a Delaware beach or down to Ocean City, or take a train to New York and do god knows what. He'd only know where she'd been if he saw a matchbook.

"You'll wind up dead in an alley one of these days, Sunny," he told her once, knowing it was a mistake to mention it.

She had laughed. "Yes, probably in an opium den on Third Avenue, lizards crawling on the ceiling. Why don't you ever pursue me, Fletcher?"

He left the office walking briskly down the marble steps which he still found impressive and began walking to Floyd's. He was tired and his stomach was in a knot. Tidwell had gone on a tirade about Sunny before he left.

"If it weren't for those canceled checks, I'd never know she was alive. I hope you'll let me know if she dies," he'd shouted to Fletcher, which was as close as he ever came to mentioning that he knew about them. "God preserve you from ungrateful daughters," he'd shouted toward the empty staff room outside his office in case there was someone still there to know he was once more declaiming his daughter who was an embarrassment to him.

Fletcher had heard the charges against Sunny again and again.

"There used to be an old man lived down the road from us back home," the congressman had said, "lived in one of those possum trot houses with a hole in the middle and a tire swing in the front—he had ten daughters. I asked him one time, I said, 'Mr. Hawthorne, don't you ever now and then wish you could send one of them girls back and get you a good boy?' and he said, 'I tell you, Cap, I wouldn't trade a one of them'— every one of them ugly as the side of a barn—'Now a son he'll go running off joining the army and getting smart and telling you how to bait your hook, but a daughter's respectful and a comfort to a man in his old age. Why, I'll have biscuits every morning of my life,' he said.

"But me . . . all my life I try to get ahead and work hard and educate my child and make a good living and give her a position she could be proud of, and what does she do but run off and live like a bum? The minute her mother dies, she runs off.

"She was a beautiful little girl, Fletcher," he'd say nostalgically. "When she went off to college she wrote us beautiful letters. Then when I wouldn't let her go to art school she quit writing."

Tidwell was getting old. Nowadays there was dandruff on his shoulders and his dress was getting more and more sloppy, like an unkempt old man's. Often his conversation was disconnected and his stories were always about the past.

"But letter writing can get out of hand. Now I knew a man one time, lived out by O'Donnell, had a daughter who went way off to college, somewhere in Florida, and she was a big letter writer, been a big letter writer all her life. When she was a kid she'd write the ice cream man letters. But she went off to school and like lots of kids who go off to school she got strange notions. She began signing her letters home with her whole name just like she did her letters to strangers. She started writing dead people she was supposed to be studying

47

about, and before long she was writing dead relatives and sending the letters to graveyards—Aunt Julia Peabody, Evergreen Cemetery, Borger, Texas."

Fletcher had laughed as Tidwell expected him to, thinking what a son-of-a-bitch he was but liking him, too.

Inside Floyd's Fletcher ordered a beer and a chicken-fried steak and tried to phone Sunny again. There was still no answer.

"Hi ya doing?" Claudine called to him. She was wearing gold stretch pants and talking to three guys in motorcycle jackets at the bar.

Claudine had been running Floyd's for four years since her husband died of emphysema after living six years with only one lung. Now and then old friends came in and she'd talk about him and bring out the phtoograph she kept in the cash register drawer of him in a World War II Seabees uniform.

Fletcher ate the meal too quickly and ordered another beer and tried to phone again and got no answer. He walked back to his table hating himself for being in Washington in the first place and for his naïveté in believing Tidwell that he was needed, that he would have effect. He saw himself as simply one in a procession of enthusiastic fools who came with illusions only to find himself in the same box answering the same questions the same way Tidwell had done for years. In the end you fitted the slot or you were ejected.

Alma, the go-go dancer, wandered in wearing a too tight sweater over a too tight skirt that bunched up around her waist.

"Have a beer," he offered. "I thought this was your night off."

"Isn't that a bitch," she said. "Nowhere to go on your night off but where you work."

Beneath the glasses and the false eyelashes one of her eyes

wandered slightly. She sat down and carefully worked a cigarette into a rhinestone holder.

"Where's the girl?"

"Ran off with a truck driver," Fletcher said.

"Oh, you're putting me on. I figure you two gonna get
married and have a nice house in the suburbs and kids."

"We look like that, huh?" But he saw she had meant it as
a compliment.

He lighted her cigarette and she propped her arms on the
table, her hands crossed before her face. Fletcher noticed that
she had beautiful arms.

"Oh, I don't believe in marriage. I believe in the Biblical
way of concubines."

She smiled and blew smoke from her nose and mouth at
once. "I don't believe in it either. I've been married once," she
said. "Burned once . . . you know. Of course, I still get
engaged now and then, but I don't know . . ." She pulled
her orange overdrawn lips into a thin line and smiled sadly.
"People don't seem to have happy marriages like they used to.
I think it's men. Men are different. Maybe women are
different—meaner. My mama and daddy were married forty-
two years. Forty-two years with the same person, can you
imagine!"

Fletcher ordered himself a beer and ordered Alma a Pepsi.

"There was one I mighta been happy with. He was tough. I
shoulda married him. . . . You might not believe it but I
weighed one hundred and sixty pounds once. I was late losing
my baby fat, some girls are like that, you know. Well, I was
really wild about this fellow. He was a truck driver," she said.
"A big fat wop. I've always kinda gone for heavy men. They
feel so good and solid when you put your arms around them.
And they put an arm around you and you feel like somebody's
got a hold of you, know what I mean?" Fletcher said not

exactly and she laughed and knocked her ashes off in the ashtray carefully and inhaled and blew the smoke out her nose as she talked. "Well, he went on a job and was gone a long time and I went on a diet. I mean I really fasted. I suffered. I didn't eat anything but prune yogurt and grapefruit and now and then a piece of meat. And I took milk of magnesia, I mean the whole bit, you know. Well, he called when he got outside Winston-Salem, where we was living, and I got all dressed up like Gina Lollobrigida, who he worshiped next to the Virgin Mary, and there I was spread out on the couch all excited, and he walks in the door and takes one look at me and don't say nothing. After a minute he just says, 'Let's eat!'

"So he takes off his shirt and goes into the kitchen and fixes up this big pot of spaghetti and sets it in front of me and says 'Eat!' Well, I just picked up my skinny self and took that plate of spaghetti and goes 'whomp' right into his lap. And I got up from there and packed my suitcases and that's when I came to D.C. Heavenly father, was I mad!" She looked over Fletcher's shoulder at Claudine laughing with one of the motorcycle guys. "He was jealous—ugh, was he jealous! But he was a good guy. I was just a kid. . . . He was a real man, I'll say that for him. Most of the men nowadays . . . I don't know. . . . I shoulda married him. . . . That was a turning point, you know. Sometimes I wonder—a million times I've wondered about if I'd a stayed there . . ."

She pulled her cigarette stub out of the holder and dropped it in the ashtray, and sat looking at the empty rhinestone holder.

"Oh, you'd probably be fat now," Fletcher said.

She seemed relieved to laugh. She threw her head back and laughed too loudly. "Yeah, that's right," she said, "I sure as hell would be fat." She rose as though that thought had made her body heavier. "Nice talking to ya. Thanks for the Pepsi."

He watched her walk over to one of the motorcycle men

who had thick, greasy, blonde hair and wore a soft black cap with a visor. He put a tattooed hand on her arm.

We all try over and over, Fletcher thought. Over and over and maybe sometimes, if we're lucky, we learn a little something.

He drank another beer and decided he'd go back to the office and work.

Walking back down Independence he felt a lot better. The Capitol dome rose in the darkness casting a golden glow like some giant illuminated wedding cake.

Father Timothy Rose lived in an old office building awaiting demolition with Xed windows. He and Sunny climbed the four flights to his room up the sagging wooden stairs strewn with wilted flowers.

"The sign of Louie," the priest said, pointing to the flowers, explaining that Louie lived in the hall and worked part time as a florist delivery man whenever he was sober enough. "He's a good man," the priest said, "he loves flowers. I think he must have been raised on a farm. Sometimes he thinks he's grown them."

On the second floor landing they passed the crumpled army blanket and pillow where Louie slept. His other possessions were in a cardboard box nearby. Propped against the wall were three dry wine bottles of dead gladiolas and the thin spidery skeletons of fern.

"What happened to him?" Sunny asked.

"I don't know. He says he had a wife once. . . . Sometimes in the night he sings hymns, strange, crude hymns about blood."

There was a big padlock on the priest's door. The room smelled of sweat and incense. It was a large, tall-ceilinged old office room with a small folding bed, a wooden office chair stripped of rollers and a file cabinet topped with personal effects and used for a bureau. There was a basin in the corner and a coat rack holding a small assortment of black clothes and white rumpled shirts and collars. A wastebasket turned upside down had been made into a sort of altar with a white cloth spread across the top and a crucifix standing in the middle. There was a guitar in a corner and a scatter of magazines and books on the floor. All the objects were at one end of the room around a window which looked down on a five-minute car wash and beyond that an underpass with railroad tracks on top that ran diagonal to the view. A sign on the side of the road said "Turn on lights before entering."

Father Rose offered her a pipe with a few threads of pot, which she declined, and then opened a bottle of scotch that stood beside the bed. "It is one of the legacies of my religious training," he said. "I learned to drink good scotch." He rinsed two glasses in the basin, poured the scotch and added a bit of water.

After throwing some underwear on the floor beneath it, he offered her the small bed and sat himself on the swivel chair. Sunny slipped off her huaraches and pulled her legs up beside her on an old red Indian blanket that reminded her of high school necking blankets. She sat gratefully leaning against the wall. From the window came the soft flutter of pigeons on the roof above.

"Why did you become a priest?" she asked.

He leaned back in the wooden executive chair and looked at the ceiling thoughtfully. "It was an hereditary disease passed from my grandfather. He was born in Ireland and was very religious, also very hungry and thirsty. He entered the church to eat. Then he ran away to America with my grandmother and settled in a Chicago slum. They had twelve children and each time he touched her he believed he was blaspheming God. He would pray and scream and screw and beat her. He had a great gift for elaborate ranting. Once a friend and I tried to tape a fight to sell to a movie writer." He laughed and walked to the window and looked down at the street where a line of cars had queued to enter the car wash.

"There were seven daughters and one boy who survived. My father was to redeem his father's sin. Of course he ran away. But he was like his father in many ways, very loud and social and very visceral. He touched people when he talked to them. He hugged his friends. He wanted to be an artist but he drank till his hands shook. He ran my mother off so I lived with my grandparents. Every night my grandfather would pray over me to become a priest. . . ."

He opened a drawer of the file cabinet, which Sunny could see was filled with bottles of liquor. He removed a small sack and proceeded to scatter seed on the windowsill for the pigeons.

"My grandmother suffered a great deal. He broke her pelvis once and she never walked right after that. Once we were playing 'My Ship Comes Loaded' and my grandmother said, 'My ship comes loaded and sinks.'" He laughed and finished his drink, put the sack back in the file and poured himself another. He sat down in the chair facing her and leaned back watching the pigeons.

"I was happy in the seminary for a while," he said. "It was in the country. I'd never lived in the country. It was in an old mansion. I used to daydream I was rich and lived there. And as long as it was daylight I could believe in what I was doing, but at night, when I was alone with myself in the darkness, knowing myself . . . I decided one night I had always thought of God as a great gray blob. A great gray blob sprayed with flock like a movie monster. The first night I realized that I ran out into the hall laughing. I was given some demerits for causing a disturbance and being up after lights out. . . ."

He leaned forward in the chair abruptly and looked toward

the window where a pigeon was pecking at the seeds and watching them with one precise, red-rimmed black eye. "I have watched carefully," he said gravely. "The idea of God seems to have nothing to do with anything on these streets. . . ."

The pigeon walked its old woman's walk to the edge of the window and flew away. Timothy Rose left the chair and sat beside her on the bed. "The people in that car wash, however, are real. I watch them. Five black men dry a car when it leaves the rinser. Five strong, black men wipe a car. Someday I will talk to them. I have a great feeling for them . . . more than I ever had for God."

He looked down at her bare foot beside him and gripped it with his hand.

"Your foot I could love more," he said.

His hand, at first gentle, began to tighten on her foot until it hurt. She watched her foot grow white around his fingers and she was at once afraid and embarrassed to look at his face. When she did she saw the discomfort and she relaxed, touching his hand with her own, and he released her, laughing lightly, and rose from the bed to fill their glasses once more. He picked up the guitar and sat back in the chair and sang.

Jesus, why are you lying there in the gutter,
Lipstick on your mouth, a pearl in your ear . . .

Why are you dragging your mother
Up the twelve flights of stairs . . .

Don't you know the children of Is-ra-el . . .
Will offer you a home someday . . .
Don't you know that every Easter
Someone, somewhere prays . . .

She stretched out on the bed listening, feeling heavy and tired, and dozed off. When she woke it was dark and the car

54

wash had closed. As she stirred he rose from the chair and lighted a candle on the file cabinet. It flickered and only vaguely lighted the room.

"You are very peaceful when you sleep," he said.

"Sometimes."

Her mouth felt dirty and brown and she took a sip of the remaining scotch from her glass. She rose and stretched and went to the window and leaned out. It was dark except for a streetlight and a few cars. The alley beside the building was littered with battered garbage cans and the entrance blocked by a small crane.

"You are a misfit, aren't you?" she called back to him. "You are a misfit, too, I should say." She turned around and sat on the window ledge.

"I simply seek to place responsibility somewhere . . . besides in chromosomes and crystalline structures and chemical reactions. We're destroying ourselves and what civilization has learned with our refusal to place responsibility. A madman—my grandfather—can live all his life without blame as long as he is not so overtly destructive as to leave his bloody victims around. Yet he probably rendered as much destruction in total number of lives and more suffering within the rhythms and cycles of his mad life than a mass murderer does in his one night or week of mania. But as long as one holds to certain routines . . ."

He raved, his strong voice battering against Sunny and the dirty walls of the room.

"Once we are all mad, as seems entirely possible, we will begin to measure destruction. . . ."

She had ceased listening to him and watched the red light of a plane dissect the disk of the moon above the railroad trestle.

"I'm in love with planes," she said when he no longer spoke.

Outside the room the sound of slow labored steps and then a knock.

"Louie," the priest announced and the door opened to a red-faced, rumpled man with a green carnation in the lapel of his long brown coat.

"Louie, this is Sunny," the priest said. "She is from the other side of the moon where planes come from."

Louie nodded to her and handed a sack to the priest. "Pleased to meet you," he said. "I have just the flowers for you," he said studying her. "I'm in the florist business. We had a good day today, Father Rose. I took some flowers downtown to a lady from her husband she'd run off and she about cried when she saw them. I told her a man who'd send eight-dollar glads when he could get six-dollar glads deserved another chance. That's the way it is in the flower business. You do lots of good, you know what I mean?"

Sunny smiled at him and nodded. There was an innocence about his red face. He started out the door and stopped. "Are there moon flowers on the moon?" he asked.

"Oh, yes," she said, "Lovely, big ones."

He nodded. "I knew there would be," he said, "no matter what the spacemen say."

The priest offered Sunny a beer and an egg roll from the sack. He moved the candle closer, hiding the far reaches of the room and making it nearly cozy. Later Louie returned and laid two gardenias before her and left without speaking as though there was a great performance in progress which he was happy to silently adorn. The gardenias were brown-tipped and yellowed but their fragrance slowly filled the room and created a soft warmth like music.

They ate quietly and sat peacefully smoking.

"I have a secret," she said, her arms gripping her stomach, feeling excited at telling him about her baby.

"That's good," he said, "I have one, too."

56

"You tell first," she said.

He finished his beer and went to the door and turned on the overhead light. The room grew ugly ocher in the electric light and it occurred to her that whatever his secret was it would not be pleasant now. He went to the basin and stood before the small round dime store mirror. He removed his coat, hanging it on the rack, and then his shirt. His skin was very white and freckled and black hair grew on his chest and back and curled over the top of his undershirt. His arms were soft and contourless, like a woman's. He took a jar from on top of the file cabinet and opened it. Sunny felt suddenly fearful of what he was going to do. With the light his talk and his manner frightened her.

"Some nights I do this," he said glancing at her. His hand moved and a black smear streaked across his forehead and then on either side of his face, his chin, his nose and neck. His hands moved with the knowingness of a middle-aged matron until his face was black and then he covered the back of his hands. He replaced his shirt and collar and coat and hung a big gold cross around his neck and faced her. He stood like a wax figure, his eyes closed, his face in total blackness, a human riddle.

She struggled to speak. "It's grotesque," she finally blurted. But it was more. To her it was hideous and a mockery. She felt as though the awful thigh-slapping white minstrels she'd seen once when she was a child were now there confronting her.

"It's obscene. You're mad!"

He turned and pulled a towel from beside the basin and began wiping his fingers slowly. "I don't know," he said. "Try to understand. You are putting yourself into what you see. It gives me a freedom that I need. It gives me a happiness and a communion. . . ." he said.

He was looking at himself in the mirror, leaning forward

staring into his blackened eyes when she left, slipping out the door and running down the stairs strewn with an occasional dying gardenia.

Fletcher, I want to say, you remember that strange priest? But Fletcher is reading. He is learning a great deal about politics. He is captured, fascinated by the raw dealing of power. He is beginning to interpret all human relations in terms of a power struggle, and to judge men by their effectiveness.

Last week he tried to convince my father that he should oppose a bill on the floor. Fletcher, my father said, it don't take long to learn in this business, that it's not wise to bare your ass unless you have to. Fletcher laughed. He admires my father's sense of self-protection. He is a politic man, he says, with that keen extra sense of how far to go and just how much to say. Fletcher now writes newsletters. He says it's a challenge to discuss a controversial subject without taking a position. It's a game of wits.

Why do you do it? I asked him.

It's my job.

But if you think it's a lie.

Not a lie, Sunny, just an evasion.

Isn't that a lie?

No, not exactly. Besides I don't know if he knows it's an evasion. I really don't know what he knows. I keep hoping to find out.

I don't know how you can work for him.

It was love brought me here, he teased.

Oh, don't give me that, I said crossly.

Look, Sunny, we've been through it before. I thought it would be interesting. I thought I might even have some influence. I thought I would learn a lot. So I've learned a lot—a lot about how impotent most of them are. That's worth something. So it's not worked out perfectly. What does? Maybe it was a mistake. I don't know. Sometimes it's worth trying.

You're implying I won't try anything.

I didn't say that.

Why does everybody act like I've never worked?

I had to laugh. He laughed and we were both relieved. We've been through all that before. Before and before and before.

Worked, indeed I have. Hotting up all those old grimy state representatives in from the farm for a while to lick the lobbyists. Demure over my typewriter. Demure smile. Demure dress. Demurely sliding away from those horny hands.

Cap Tidwell's girl, huh? She must be a hot one, that one.

Then the good social worker. Dispense a few of those dirty nickels, my dear.

All those sad faces, one after another.

You got a boyfriend? You sleep with him? He's not the father of that child? Excuse the questions. Just the regulations, you know, nothing personal. . . .

You must have a more professional approach, Miss Tidwell.

Screw you, you animal. You son of a bitch. You great rotting system of damnation.

That blind woman bitten on the ankles by the rats. Bloody rags around her legs, scattering week-old bread around her bed to keep them away.

Later getting ready for bed I tell him I have seen the priest.

A real weirdo, huh? he says yawning.

He's not really a priest, I say.

What's he, an impersonator? He laughs, buttoning his pajamas.

He's a sign, I say. He looks at me curiously and walks into the bathroom. He is a sign reminding me of things I don't want to remember, I finish to myself.

Has it ever occurred to you that when someone becomes a priest he gives himself over to being a symbol? He's not an individual anymore. Wouldn't that be awful . . . ?

Hum . . . he replies, not really interested.

Maybe that's partly why they do it, there's not enough of themselves.

Fletcher sits on the side of the bed and lights a cigarette. He runs a finger down my back making me shiver and he opens his book again. The smoke envelops the small room before it finds the open window.

I lie in bed facing the wall, thinking of my mother. Leita. Leita in a brown photo, my age, in a white batiste dress. In front of a crepe myrtle. The sun in her eyes. A shy smile. Why do I think of her like that picture? Why not like the tired, sad-eyed woman, rouged, burnt fresh from the beauty parlor. Wrinkled neck, gray old skin. Flat sausage breasts, the indignity of a padded bra at fifty. Green medicine bottles. Wandering in house slippers in the night. Always the rumpled bed. The rumpled bed where she lay most of her days for years until she stored the strength to rise and close the windows of her car, and lock the doors, and drive into the side of the underpass very much like the one outside the priest's window.

My father was away in Washington when she died. They phoned him. An accident. Serious. Serious condition . . . I nearly laughed. Had she not been in serious condition before, that she would drive her car into a concrete wall . . . ? Or was she just brave?

Relatives met him at the airport. They drove him home. She was dead.

In death dignity becomes of monumental importance. It is the only thing to grope for, because we've failed. We failed to keep her alive. We failed to keep that great blackness away from us, failed in being reminded of it. Everyone's failed. But my father failed more. The politic man was jelly.

I heard the car. Left my room to meet him, aware of a slight embarrassment that we should be stripped so helplessly of our armor. Crying, with alcohol breath, he hugged me feeling big and bear-like, my breasts pressed against the slope of his belly. He collapsed on the end of the couch, hugging me, whimpering and sobbing. He began mumbling, surrendering all the intimate struggles of their life together, the secrets of their private war.

I pulled away in horror. His friends murmured to him, oh, Cap, don't, but they listened, they heard. He sat on the big brown couch running his fingers along the cording on the arm, his hat still on his head and cried, his dribbling mouth shattering her dignity as completely as her small body had been broken a few hours before.

His grief opened up some primitive instinct for destruction. It moved into rage. He went to her room, opened all the drawers, pulled out her clothes, held them against his face crying into them, and then ripped them apart. Her shredded clothing piled on the bed and spilled on the floor, desecrated, until I screamed.

You don't care, he said. You don't care, you don't care.

Later he demanded I get her rings. I used words to him I had never used except in my mind. I thought he would hit me. Kill me. He got the gun. Go get the rings. . . .

I swear to God I'll never set foot in the same house with you again . . . never, never, never.

Her fingers were like wax.

Fletcher stabs his cigarette and closes his book. He goes to the window and looks out at the overcast sky as he does each night. He has rituals to ease him into the night. He puts a wash cloth under the faucet drip in the basin, crawls into bed and turns off the light. He gives a tired sigh and I turn toward him raising my shoulders for his arm to slip under me.

III

Friday night. At a drive-in movie with a blanket wrapped around them, half a case of beer, hot dogs, popcorn. Sunny in a poncho, her waist swollen. It's ponchos from here on out, world.

"I'll call you Sun-in-the-face," Fletcher says.

Sunny could not remember when she'd been to a drive-in movie. It was wonderful: the lines of stuffed cars and station wagons with children bedded down and crawling over the backs of seats, and streaming back and forth with food and soft drinks and playing on the gym-sets beside the concession stand. There were cartoons and trailers and commercials during which cars began honking until it sounded as though the entire triangle of cars had joined in protest.

It was a doublebill horror show. The two high school couples next to them necked, gradually slipping down in the seats.

"Do you think anybody's watching the movie?" Sunny asked.

"I am," Fletcher said, chewing on popcorn. She laughed,

took a handful of popcorn and turned to the movie. A monster was terrorizing a girls' dormitory. The local populace was organizing to attack the monster.

"I'm not going to watch the end, monsters always die," Sunny said turning away.

On the other side of them a mother was slapping her kids in the back seat. There was a cacophony of cries.

Fletcher put his arms around Sunny and patted her stomach. The music was building as the search for the monster continued. Behind them a car engine started and the wheels spun gravel as it drove down the aisle.

"I've been thinking about naming this child Charlemagne," Fletcher said.

"Actually I'd planned to name this child Zacchaeus," Sunny said.

"Oh, that's got a real sexy ring to it. What if it's a girl? Zachy?"

"Zachilisha."

"Now that's an interesting name. Biblical, no doubt, you being so devout and all."

"Absolutely. . . ." She sang, clashing with the search music:

> Zacchaeus was a wee little man, and a wee little man was
> he . . .
> He climbed up in a sycamore tree for the Lord he wanted
> to see . . .
> And as the Savior passed that way and He looked up in
> the tree,
> He said, Zacchaeus, come down from there,
> For I'm going to your house today.

"Charming," Fletcher said.

"I knew you'd like it," Sunny grinned.

The woman next to them was staring threateningly, her children crying quietly in the back.

"Poor Zacchaeus."

"Why poor Zacchaeus?"

"Well, he was a rich publican and probably short and aggressive."

"Oh, he was probably potent as hell," Fletcher said. "Wonder how they climbed trees in those robes?"

"You're certainly silly enough to be the father of Zacchaeus," Sunny laughed and leaned against him.

On the screen a girl and football star were staggering through a swamp trying to escape the monster. The search party was miles away.

"I hope the monster catches them," Sunny said. "I like the monster best. His antennae are kinda cute, don't you think?"

Fletcher opened another beer and handed it to her. He tried to make a face like the monster and growled at her cross-eyed, bringing his hands to her throat.

"Would you look at the couples next to us," she whispered giggling.

Fletcher made a face and dangled his hands monster-like toward the front seat couple watching them.

He turned back and swallowed some beer. "Look," he said seriously, turning to Sunny, "why don't you quit acting noble? The least we could do is get married. This kid is going to have problems enough being a short republican named Zacchaeus."

"You do make a good monster," she said. "Look, they fell down in the swamp. She didn't get her hair messed up, though."

He slid his hand under the poncho. "Why don't we go home and play monster?" he said.

They dropped the speaker putting it on the rack and Sunny

waved goodbye to the cars on either side of them before they left.

They drove to town, Fletcher singing . . .

Why don't you love me like you used to, Sunny,
How come you treat me like a worn-out bunny?
My hair is still kinky and my eyes are still runny,
Why don't you love me like you used to, Sunny . . .

"Listen, Sunny," Fletcher called to her in the kitchen where she was fixing drinks, "I have bad news."

She was running water over the bottom of an ice tray, watching the frost dissolve. He sounded serious and she guessed what he was about to say before he said it.

"You've been chosen an astronaut!" she said.

"I've got to go to the farm this weekend."

"Oh, shit," she said. All the ice plopped into the sink.

"What's wrong with being an astronaut?"

She watched the ice cubes fall away from the metal skeleton and slide toward the drain.

"You'd have to go into training and you might float into outer space without me," she said.

"Why don't you come?"

She dropped cubes into the two jelly glasses and poured bourbon.

"No, thanks," she called. "No, thank you very much," she repeated, entering the room and handing him a glass. "I'd as soon float off into outer space. . . . When are you going?"

"I don't know."

"That means tonight," she said, sitting down in the overstuffed chair and swinging her legs over the side. She felt the crossness build inside her.

"It means I don't know," he said.

They were quiet. The water faucet dripped and she circled

66

the ice round and round in her glass. Fletcher rose and turned on the record player.

Shut up, she told herself, don't say anything more, but the annoyance was a volcano inside her.

"Well, it seems reasonable you'll go tonight or in the morning. . . . By all means don't let me stand in your way." She brought her poncho up to cover her face. "I'm just a stoic Indian lady."

"Look, you know he works lots of weekends when he's here. It's a fact. Why fight about it every time? We might as well get used to it and work something out."

She let the poncho fall from her face. "Why do you always wait till the last minute to tell me . . . ?"

"Because I don't know until the last minute," he said.

"He just gave you a message via mental telepathy?"

Now you've done it, she told herself, watching his face change to real anger and then looking away.

"All my life I've had to live with everything changing at the last minute, why should I have to live like that now?" she asked, making what she knew was a futile jab for sympathy.

"If you want to live with me, you'll live like that," he said, with a cold control she detested.

The record, on automatic, played on. . . .

Ain't nobody . . . gonna turn me around no more . . .
Ain't nobody . . . gonna turn me around . . .
Well, I've learned my lesson and now I see
Love ain't the th-in-g for me . . .
Ain't nobody . . . gonna turn me around . . . turn me
    around . . .

She took a long drink. The bourbon stung her throat going down and left a sweet aftertaste. She felt calm and detached and determined as the song. Let it alone, she told herself, but she couldn't; she didn't want to stop badly enough. Something inside pushed her along as steadily as the record, something wanting to hurt him.

"I know all about his working weekends. All those people he invites, that shifting menagerie of blowhards and conventioneers. . . . He never really gets any work done. . . . I'm sure you'll find a companion . . . or maybe he'll give you permission to come back in for tomorrow night. . . ." She bent over, burying her face in her arms. Oh, what a lovely girl, she told herself, what a lovely, lovely girl.

Fletcher finished his drink and stood up. She could feel him looking down at her hatefully.

"If you weren't pregnant, I swear to god I'd knock the shit out of you."

She heard him move away and the sound of the closet door closing and the duffle bag being pulled out and the drawers sliding open and shut.

She raised her head and watched him. The crossness was gone, exhausted.

"I'm sorry," she said. "I shouldn't have said that."

He slammed a drawer shut and faced her.

"You know the difference between you and a bitch is sometimes you say you're sorry afterward."

She met his eyes and there was nothing there for her. Nothing.

He threw a pair of socks at her and she caught them and held them in her hands as though they were interesting.

"You let yourself say *anything* that comes into your selfish head and then you think saying you're sorry makes it all right. Well, you know, it doesn't always work like that." He zipped up the bag and crossed the room.

She was suddenly terribly afraid to be alone.

"I may be dead when you get back."

"It's too late to joke."

"I'm not joking," she said, her voice muffled by the socks she held to her face.

He put his coat on, not looking at her. "I'll take my chances," he said and left, slamming the door.

She listened for the gate and the car door and the engine, hoping he'd come back. When she heard the car turn the corner, she threw the socks on the floor and made herself another drink.

✑

His voice always there just at the edge of her mind.

. . . god damned self-righteous young . . . don't know what it used to be like, how much better it is. . . .

He drifts on a blue plastic float in the pool, his white stomach rising like a burial mound, a beer wrapped in a wash cloth set in a metal ring attached to the float, his head resting in his hands, his white fish underarms bare to the sun. He kicks a foot, water splashes glittering in the sun and falls across his old man's legs. . . . He splashes again . . . the water sprinkles on his stomach . . . he spreads the droplets over the mound . . . his hands move drowsily. . . .

. . . they ordered the electric chair and started saving up people. . . . like a state fair . . . fried white men first . . . three of 'em . . . the first night . . . fried thirteen niggers one after another . . . had to go outside and puke. . . .

The sun behind a cloud . . . come out here, Leita . . . look like a damn Jew in a camp . . . local red neck standing in the cemetery charging a dime . . . see the burn marks . . .

The plastic float hangs in the center of the pool, a bulbous stopper in the sparkling center. . . . head laid to the side, eyes closed, like dead . . . going down the drain . . .

Come out in the sun, Leita. . . .

Into the kitchen to find another drink . . . drink, drink to stop me think . . . come along with me, little bottle. . . .

Lovely overstuffed chair abandoned in the streets. We dragged it home, pushed it through the window, broke the glass, both of us sitting in it, carving a hole in the arm stuffing, the Round Rock ashtray to fit therein . . . from the Sam Bass Cafe. . . . Poor Sam, a new gravestone for Sam, the other one all chopped up by tourists. . . . Here I have brought you to this historic site, the grave of Sam Bass for the auspicious occasion of proposing marriage. . . . Sharing all my worldly goods . . . Why, these shoes . . . twenty dollars . . . one blue-jean jacket . . . half a bottle of Jack Daniels, one thirty-gauge shotgun and a domino set. . . .

Play a game of dominoes, Sunny child? . . .

Oh happy day when I was born . . .

Why do you do it, Daddy, all that corny playing hymns and carrying the flag and all that marching music, and making mother and me sit up there on the platform dressed up . . . ?

The people . . . they see that flag a-waving and their chests swell . . . and they hear that music a-pounding and their hearts pump . . . and they see us sitting up here looking good and smiling, and suddenly all that chest swelling and heart pumping is us sitting up there looking purty and they love us. . . .

Sunny, you shouldn't drink like that . . . common, like your father. . . .

Don't my daughter talk good when she's drunk. . . .

White pinafores and Mary Jane shoes on platforms . . . Mama in blue . . .

Marry in blue your love is true, Sunny. . . .

Wear your Brownie costume . . . a girl scout would look good on the platform . . . put on your majorette costume and twirl, Sunny . . . you gotta let that skirt out a bit . . . laughing . . . twirling on the platform, Daddy!

My Daddy says . . . six inches longer. . . . I know the other girls. . . .

Fletcher, I wanna go with you. . . .

Somewhere in the closet. Standing, swaying, pulling a chair, caught on the closet, dumb chair . . . somewhere packed away. The room sways like this always? . . . clutching the side . . . on a shelf tucked away, yes, carefully surrounded by tissue paper, the way mother tries to put things away . . . trying to put some order in our lives, Sunny. . . .

The white satin has yellowed. The boots wrapped separately in plastic paper, polished, feel the white Shinola. Every Sunday white polished shoes, don't rub your shoes against your socks that way, Sunny. . . .

Unzipped jeans, poncho off, everything . . . all these clothes on the floor . . . what a mess . . . from the closet . . . naked . . . and fat in the waist, my dear . . . the satin cool against my skin . . . cool, pin the braid on one shoulder, pull it up . . . arms in the sleeves . . . thinner now . . . the feel of the satin . . . all those dark, frightened nights, cold uneven ground, a swallow of whiskey in the restroom, giggling girls, sitting afterwards, vain . . . country boys in cowboy hats smiling . . . college boys with pipes, pins, big things in their pants, bottles in their pockets . . . snuggling on the back seats in the cold, passing the bottle to warm the hands running down the white satin. . . .

I'll use it as a wedding dress, Fletcher . . . twirl down the aisle on my daddy's arm . . . a side twirl . . . never very good at that, either. . . .

Button . . . button . . . button the bodice . . . zip up the side . . . zip, god damn it, breathe in, oh mermaid, with the swollen waist . . . monster, monster, who is the monster? . . .

One good yank . . .

Oh, god damn it . . . god damn it . . . pull it down

quick . . . falling on the couch . . . holding the torn side
. . . zipped skin, white like scales, scraped . . . god damn it
hurts. . . .

The couch dips . . . the room spins . . . hang on, oh girl
monster . . . oh, no, you can't lose me, not yet . . . I can't
throw up here, bathroom too far . . . cry . . . cry . . .
that'll be enough . . . cry into the satin. . . .

Still singing . . .

. . . you've been so doggone mean . . .
You've thrown out every one of my dreams . . .
You've turned me around . . . stone around . . . turned
me around . . .

She dreamed she was insane, her vision all beige and nar-
rowed to an area no broader than a tiny television screen.
There was no sound, only the beige faces of people laughing.
When she could not escape, her body responded to their jeers
by disintegrating.

She lay back for a moment, frightened. It happens all the
time. It's probably better. She closed her eyes. If I should die
before I wake I pray the Lord my soul to take. She had not
thought of the prayer in years. She pulled herself up and sat
on the edge of the couch. It's better, she told herself. Don't
think any more. Blood. God damn it. Can anything good
come out of Tarsus? She nearly laughed.

She threw a blanket over the couch and went to the bathroom. In the mirror she looked gaunt and blotched. Fluores-
cent lights are meany things. I will brush my teeth so they
may glimmer when I die. And now this word from our
sponsor. My name is Sunny Tidwell from Rising Star, Texas
and I had the cleanest teeth in the hospital when I died.

She pulled on her jeans. Somewhere a blouse. Now the
raincoat.

72

Outside it was cold and the street was deserted.

My god, I've got to walk to the avenue and get a cab. She turned around and went back inside and got the bottle of bourbon and wrapped it in her poncho. How's that for a baby?

Outside she felt her stomach falling. She sat down on the steps.

Now think, think, think, me girl. You stand up. Move down the sidewalk. One foot in front of the other. One at a time. No one will bother you. Who wants a bleeding, bitchy girl? Fletcher said so. Walk down the sidewalk, cross the street, down one more block to the avenue. Stand there, stout, your father's daughter, strong in the face of great obstacles, a real profile in coarseness you.

She stood up, wavering slightly. Who's drunk. Drunk? Too scared. Scared and drunk. Make your legs move. The houses began to move past slowly.

Yea, though I walk through the valley of the shadow of death, I will fear no evil for thou art with me, thy rod and thy staff they comfort me . . . surely goodness and mercy will follow me all the days of my life and I will dwell in the house of the Lord . . .

Where's my rod and staff? If I just had a rod and staff. Hello, all you sleeping, sleepy people screwing up there in the dark. . . .

She passed a corner grocery . . . the drink that makes you think . . . he sells one-cent wax-people candies, you bite off the heads, drink the colored water inside, and chew them.

There was no one on the street, only a car or two passing on the avenue ahead. Somewhere a cat yowled.

Walk, walk, walk. Great progress, my dear. Only a block now. Don't hit me crossing this street, any of you invisible cars. How many points for bleeding pregnant women?

She felt her stomach fall again and the warm dampness between her legs. She stopped and leaned against a fence and unfurled the bottle and lifted it to her mouth. Her hands were trembling. What if I lie down here under that tree and die? It would be easier, maybe I'd bleed quietly to death. That doesn't hurt, does it? I'd just drink all this and go to sleep. Good idea . . . no, no . . .

Walk, walk a few more houses. So dark along here, right before the avenue, the trees hanging over you like that, clutching at you, maybe it's only the bottle they want. Maybe they're bloodsucking trees . . . get away, you monsters.

She reached the corner and leaned against a mailbox.

Red, white, and blue. What if I crawl inside and mail myself there? What a surprise for some mailman.

There was not a car, not a cab. She stood waiting, praying.

Down the block she watched two black men approaching, cross the street . . . One in a black leather coat, round sunshades, good looking . . .

"Hey, baby," he said as he passed, "what you doing out this time of night . . . ?" They passed and wandered up the street glancing back . . . She watched them disappear wondering why she didn't cry out to them.

She hugged the bottle, dizzy, afraid she might pass out. She staggered slightly stepping out into the street.

If I just sit down here in the street, what will happen? Surely someone will stop. Nobody sits Indian style in the street. Only for dead people, shot people with holes in them to lie on. . . .

The cab was driving very fast when it passed. It had three men in it, but she raised her hand before she saw them. The driver threw on his brakes, backed up and stopped beside her.

The tall man in front of her looked halfway familiar . . . taking her arm . . . pulling on her. . . . The radio was so loud . . .

Okay you soul folks out there, if you wanna really know

where the action is, baby, you come to the Run-Around
Lounge out on Georgia Avenue . . .

What are you saying to me, I don't understand. . . .

I met a man passing out cards to the Run-Around Lounge
. . . a wild Afro hairdo and a white ruffled shirt and boots,
and he was with a white girl in a black backless dress and they
danced and he watched her . . .

Otis was singing . . . Poor Otis. Poor dead Otis. You
might have been the only man for me. You or some cat in the
Run-Around Lounge who I'll never see. Oh, made a rhyme,
see my boyfriend 'fore bedtime. . . .

Oh, no, no, no, kind man, I get your message. Strong, am I?
The police car stopped behind the cab.

"What's going on here . . . ?"

"Trying to help this lady . . . sitting in the street. . . ."

Hysterical, she staggered toward the policeman, the blood
running down her legs.

She tried to tell him she wanted to get to a hospital. . . .
She leaned against him looking into his black face . . . his
eyes cold. . . . He smelled of Old Spice . . . how could he
be a cop . . . his arm around her. . . .

"She says she's a member of Congress

.

.
"
.

An object. A dark cocoon of pain, curtained off, hidden by
duck while the dark cave which is me oozes, waiting for something to die within. There is white and metal all around,
pressing me. The pillow is stiff, starched, wounding my cheek.

Beyond the duck walls other voices. Victims of their own
caves, subject to unannounced intrusions and regulated by
dissolving buttons and needles. Mounted they lie on their

antiseptic thrones, tubes running from their bodies into glass jars on the floor—chemistry sets. Their brains escape into a black box perched on a platform in the center. Their suffering creates a camaraderie unlike the outside where friendless ladies dress up and talk over coffee cups. Cigarette smoke rises over the duck curtains in variegated billows. One rises, walks down the hall, thin swan-white legs, limp striped bathrobe, hair pressed flat in back.

Outside my window is a dull sun. It is cool, a nurse says. I lean from the bed and the gentle lines dissect the world for me, netting the concrete below, breaking my mind's fall, barred already by pain and white and the antiseptic smell that has me drugged.

They got in there and saw there was nothing they could do, she was so far gone, so they just sewed her up. . . . That Mrs. Owens down the hall . . .

I escape by singing songs in my mind. Last night aloud. The nurse jabbing my arm and then quiet, dizzy floating peace.

I wait, wait, wait. Turn. Knees raw from turning. Carts pushed. Sturdy brick nurses striding down the hall in bulldog shoes. Clean hands. Substantial watches. Shifts. On, off. On, off. Like me. On, off. On, off.

In the night the bleeding becomes worse. They carry it away and I am afraid I will die. But I am afraid to mention it. No one dies in a hospital, stupid, I tell myself, not of something like this. Oh, yes, didn't I read . . .

Do people know when they are dying? In movies they do. Do people ever scream I'm dying, I'm dying, and then don't? I might sometime. It would be just my luck to have a death scene and not die.

The pain grows. It is consuming me.

After a while they stand around and whisper, and I am wheeled away into a room with knives in glass cases, a bright light overhead. They inject peace and I drift away relieved. Whatever it was is gone, whatever growing, cropped, whatever alive, dead, removed to decay. All of it is over. I am just myself again.

Timothy Rose passed through the duck curtains, his face calm and serene as though the hospital were a refuge for him.

"I saw you on the admittance list," he said. He took her hand in his damp palm and touched her forehead sympathetically. He showed neither surprise nor curiosity at seeing her there. She pulled her hand away and he looked around at the cold, ugly accouterments of the ill surrounding her and sighed. "It's a cruel indignity," he said.

She had no desire to talk. She felt groggy, in a state of half-life, her body adjusted to a gentle hum of bare existence. She would have been content to sleep forever.

Oh, Timothy Rose, don't make me talk.

"This place isn't so bad," he said. "At least you don't have to bribe the attendants. If you were black you'd be in a ward where there were fifty beds and people dying around you. Some people even like it here. They don't have to feel responsible for themselves."

"Why are you here?" she asked.

"I come to perform my priestly duties. I make a lot of contacts this way. This is one of the few places people will talk about God. And now and then I pick up a dollar or two. . . ."

"That's sick," she mumbled.

"Sometimes in kindness I talk about God. It's a strong habit with me. It gives them comfort even if it's a lie."

She turned away facing the wall, but he took no notice.

"Of course, you are young," he said sighing, "you have little patience with momentary ease. As you grow older, you'll find some kind of momentary kindness is about all you can offer anyone. If it happens to be a lie, it's as true as anything else anyway. . . . "

"I'll never get that old," she said.

He laughed at her and turned away to stare out the window. He had not shaved and his pitted cheeks were hidden by the black stubble. In profile his features were rounded.

"The nurse told me why you are here," he said.

It's better, she wanted to say, but she was too tired. If it had been born, it might have been deformed . . . or retarded. It might have been dead. It might have been schizophrenic. It might grow awhile and have been molested or have run away or been run down by a car at an intersection. Years would pass and I would love it or hate it and it might hate me, but it would be more and more of my life only to be killed in another cruel, stupid war, or blown up accidentally by a bomb. And if it survived, why? Would it be worth it taking all those chances? Another person going through it all again. Starting all over, learning the same things, the same hurts, the same disillusionments, the same mean tricks of self-protection, of un-loving, contributing to the gross national product or sapping the welfare rolls, one more great American consumer and moviegoer.

Timothy Rose watched her with clear eyes.

"It doesn't matter," she said. "I'm tired. I'm only twenty-six and I'm tired; too tired to raise a kid." She counted the metal loops that held the duck curtain. There were fourteen. Fourteen loops on a metal pole. If each one were a year, how long it would be! She closed her eyes. "It exhausts me to think that every person has to start at the beginning. There's no progress. It's the same struggle again and again so the thought of someone else, just makes me tired. . . . "

"But there's so much hope in the beginning. . . ."

"Don't say that," she muttered. "It always dies sooner or later."

He stood up and helped himself to a drink of water from the metal pitcher. "Would you like for me to push the curtain back more so you can watch the television?" he asked jovially.

She lay with her eyes closed, not replying. Go to hell, Timothy Rose. You have the bedside manner of a head nurse. You look like a great ugly blackbird.

He pulled the chair over so that he could watch a program for a while. She was asleep when he came to the bed and leaned toward her, speaking very gravely. "I have discovered a strange thing," he said. "Do you think it possible to combine a state of dreams with consciousness?"

"That doesn't make sense," she said, struggling to stay awake.

"Lots of times I have waked from dreams but not really admitted it and continued what was really a daydream trying to persuade myself it was the dream continuing. But it was controlled by me, creating what I wanted to happen. Everyone does that, probably. But this is different. I think I've experienced a new time, a mingling of consciousness and unconsciousness that is involuntary."

"Do you have a cigarette?" she interrupted.

He stopped and dutifully removed cigarettes and lighted them. She lay back and watched the smoke from her mouth flow upward over the duck curtains to meet that outside.

"When I am very tired," he whispered, "there is a time between sleep and consciousness when the mind is awake but the unconscious has overtaken part of the brain so that the unconscious superimposes images and sounds over the conscious thoughts. It is beyond control. It occurs just this side of sleep when I am particularly tired. It is like a collage of wakefulness and dream secrets. It is hazardous. Usually," he said,

"I am shocked awake by what I have seen and heard. It is like being mad. . . ."

He held his hand to his head and the smoke from his cigarette circled him. "There are new things here," he said pressing his head. "There are many things we haven't discovered. We have to watch, remain accessible, like an investor waiting for an opportunity. There is more to our experience than we know." He looked out the window at the opposite red brick hospital wall. "It is important that we believe in the possibilities."

He smiled at her, waiting for some response, but she only closed her eyes, exhausted by him.

He took her cigarette from her fingers gently. "I am sorry," he said. "Please take care." And quietly he left the room.

Sunny slept with no sense of time, waking once to pick at a bowl of jello on a tray. She let the jello dissolve in her mouth, wondering if Timothy Rose had really been there. She tried to remember what he said, but she fell asleep again, dreaming of voices whose bodies were simple objects she could not identify. It was a troublesome, fitful dream. When she woke later the tray was gone, but there was still the television sound, and the talk of the women and the sound of one or another of them shuffling across the plastic tile floor to the bathroom.

. . . didn't find her till this morning . . . somebody broke in . . . like to beat her to death . . .

It seemed much later, another day, when Fletcher stood beside her. She opened her eyes, turned over and doubled a pillow under her head. It was nearly dark outside and raining.

Fletcher looked tired and gray-faced and hung-over. There were flecks of dried blood on his chin.

"My god, why didn't you tell me where you'd gone," he said.

She looked down at the mound where her feet were and watched the sheet wrinkle when she wiggled her toes.

"I didn't know where I was going."

"Why didn't you phone?"

"I didn't think about it. . . ."

Fletcher grimaced, removed his raincoat and draped it over the end of the bed, and lighted a cigarette. "What happened?" he asked.

She took his cigarette out of his hand and took a long draw and handed it back to him. Her mouth felt fuzzy.

"Well, this is a sort of very exclusive beauty spa where they plant flowers in your uterus. I've chosen violets, and marigolds for my ears."

He stared at her a minute, his face glum and annoyed. "Try again," he said quietly.

She saw his hand holding the cigarette tremble and she began to cry silently, great hot tears rolling down her face and hanging on her chin before they dropped onto the stiff sheet.

He sat down and took her hand and held it to his face and said he was sorry.

She felt awake for the first time and aware of her body.

There is a great wound running down the middle and across my head and circling me so that I must be careful and not move quickly or my body will fall apart into pieces.

She pulled a tissue out of the drawer of the bedside table and blew her nose.

"Tomorrow I'll be a cheerleader again, but today I'm feeling sorry for myself. And I don't know why. It's a relief in lots of ways."

"I'm sorry I was gone," he said.

"Well, when your nation calls . . ."

She wanted to pull the words back inside her, cut them out of the air, but then she was glad; she could hate herself for them.

She watched the concern disappear from his face.

Oh, god, don't be mad, Fletcher, she wanted to say. I don't want to be mean. But this isn't in the book. You look awkward and out of place and I look pale and ugly and indistinguishable from all the other ladies with hospital gowns and stainless steel water pitchers. But don't be mad! Oh, god, what's happening. This ugliness. This ugly, ugly, ugliness . . .

She caught his hand as if to stop what was happening, but he pulled away, leaving awkwardly, making an excuse to buy something.

He won't even ask questions now. He's relieved to be gone.

She tried to straighten her hair with her fingers and rub the sleep from her eyes. She swung the serving tray across the bed and opened the top where the mirror was concealed.

Will it show on my face? Will I look different? We used to think virgins looked different afterwards.

Her eyes were puffy, a little swollen, and heavy from the sedatives, but there were no wounds, no great swaths of mercurochrome, no bandages, scars, or freshly sewn incisions. She put the mirror away and looked out the window where the rain had created a pattern on the screen. She wanted to lean against the screen and feel the cool, wet on her face, and rub her cheek against the coarse metal and push. . . .

Fletcher returned with a newspaper and a bowl of roses. They were small pink sweetheart roses in a white imitation milk-glass bowl. There was a white ribbon in the middle of them, like a little girl's hair-bow. They seemed childlike and sentimental and nearly artificial. She hated them on sight, they were so sad.

She thanked him while he set them on the window against the gray space outside, against the wet void, the distant brick, the premature darkness. He sat in the metal chair and pulled out a section of the newspaper while she smoked, staring at the ceiling.

Is there nothing to say, she wondered.

"How was the weekend?" she asked finally.

"Okay," he said, not looking up from the paper. "Lots of dominoes . . . Gloria was there. . . ."

She saw them sitting around a table, pushing dominoes. Her father always railed as they played. . . . Poor black Gloria, his token, frightened of him, grateful to him . . . refilling his glasses. . . .

. . . my old mother had a woman worked for her for years, she loved old black Rose, that's what we called her, Black Rose, but once they were talking in the kitchen and Black Rose forgot herself and sat down beside Mama and Mama sprang up like a jack-in-the-box, and Black Rose was so ashamed she cried. . . . no offense, Gloria. . . .

. . . you know there's still a reward for anybody kills a bank robber . . . they wanted 'em dead, so's they wouldn't have to fool with 'em. . . . once this detective told these two nigger boys to meet him in front of the bank at a certain hour . . . so he rushed up there and shot 'em dead as a doornail . . . he got ten years. Died awhile back, didn't mention it in the paper so's not to embarrass the family. . . .

They were pushing metal carts up the hall, passing out fruit juice.

"Fletcher, there's an old woman down the hall . . . somebody came into her bedroom in the middle of the night and nearly beat her to death. She may die."

"Um . . ." he said.

"It might be catching."

"What catching?"

"Her luck . . ." If she dies her fear might still be left.

He wasn't listening.

83

When the bell rang for visitors to leave, he assembled the paper and stood up.

"Hand me the flowers, please," she asked.

He lifted the bouquet and she broke off two of the tiny roses. She pulled him toward her and ran one tiny stem through the buttonhole of his jacket. The other she stuck in her hair.

"Are you all right?" he asked. "Really?"

"I'll be all right," she said.

"When will you leave here?"

"I'll phone you," she said.

He hesitated as if there was more he wanted to say, but only kissed her lightly and left.

Later she drank her juice, carefully emptying the glass. Then one by one she broke off each rosebud and dropped it inside the glass. When the nurse came for the glass she pretended to be asleep.

Floyd's was no comfort. The Sunday night crowd seemed morose and the band was struggling with a semi-western version of "Granada." Fletcher sat in a dark corner and watched Alma swivel on the small stage. The spotlight focused below her face so that there seemed only a body with a few sequins on the midriff which sparkled occasionally. Under the blue light she looked exotic and unattainable. It was hard to reconcile the soft round undulating body with Alma. Poor Alma.

The band took a break and he watched her round bottom move back toward the ladies' room thinking how she had that sweet innocence of a real loser. There's nothing like a woman who's been kicked around, he thought. Try to love her and you find yourself beating her up in a month.

He drank a couple of beers, got a handful of change, and decided to call home. He had to wait a long time for the operator, and then there was a lot of buzzing and ringing before he finally got through.

"Yeah?" Buddy Pynes answered.

"Hey, man, what's going on?"

"Fletcher! Man, how ya doing?"

"Not bad, not bad," Fletcher said. He cracked the phone booth to get some air and the sound of the band invaded the cubicle.

"Sounds like you honky-tonking it up, boy."

"Yeah, it's always the high life here in the Capitol City. What's going on there?"

"Me and Sheila's just sitting here necking and watching Hoss Cartwright and drinking beer. I been working my ass off trying to figure out how I'm gonna make some money now that Sheila's got herself in this mess."

"What mess?" Fletcher took a drink of beer.

"Pregnant, man, I mean *with* child. Been fooling around, I believe. How're you at midwifery?"

"Oh, I knows all about birthin' babies."

They laughed.

"I told her," Buddy Pynes said, "that we ain't been married but six years, and I'm still testing her out, but she turns out to be fecund as a shad. How's it with you? Sounds like you might have a right smart of antifreeze round about."

"Well, it gets cold up here always at the end of May. Natives say it never fails."

"That right?"

"See any prospects for the Great Society down there?"

"Man, if it ain't great here, I don't know where it would be. We can get *The New York Times* on Tuesdays nowadays. They're having a goat roping this weekend over in Stella. Come down and let us show you a little culture. Might even make it to Laredo to the fights now that Sheila's in no position to run off with a matador."

"Sounds a right smart more exciting than here. Bet you don't have an Audubon Society meeting this week, though."

"Get me a beer," Buddy shouted away from the phone. "How's Sunny?"

"We're not speaking right now," Fletcher said. "She's against my running for president."

"That right?"

"I got a solution to the racial problem," Fletcher said. "Pass an amendment to the Constitution that every adult male and female of reproductive age must screw a member of the opposite race by the year 1975."

"Terrific idea, Fletcher, you'd win by a landslide."

"Yeah, that's what I thought. Maybe we could hold off this internecine warfare."

They were quiet a minute and Fletcher finished his beer.

"Please deposit another fifteen cents," the operator said.

"Well, I tell you, Buddy, be looking for some good hideouts."

"I'll do it, Fletch. You be looking for books on infant erotica. I wanna start this kid out right."

"Sure will, Bud. Good talking to you. So long."

He hung up and ordered another beer, then tried to phone another friend. While it rang he watched a kid tilting one of the pin ball machines. There was no answer so he finished the beer and went outside where it was still drizzling. He had difficulty getting his car unlocked. Not too good, he muttered to himself. Not too good.

Once outside he began driving toward town instead of his apartment. He passed dark figures walking listlessly in the rain. The radio reported rioting on Fourteenth Street the day before, and the cars of some white people had been stoned and overturned and a couple of people pulled out and beaten. There had been a shoot-out between some police and two men robbing a dairy store. One of the robbers was dead and the other in critical condition. The sixteen dollars had been recovered. There had been so many robberies the day before the police had been unable to respond to all the calls. Fletcher pulled over to the side of the curb for a police car and then for an ambulance to pass, and wondered, sitting there, whatever made him think a job, any job, would be worth this godforsaken marble city full of angry, insane, frustrated people.

He was not certain where he was going until he reached the 1950-vintage red-brick apartment house with casement windows in what was probably the only truly integrated neighborhood in the city. There was a fire hydrant beside the car when he got out, but he figured any cop with time enough to give a parking ticket in that area would be demoted for featherbedding. Why the hell do I feel so drunk, he wondered. He looked around at the gray drizzle and the dirty streets and blamed them. Contaminating my blood, he muttered to himself. A near-empty bus passed; a woman's sleeping head leaned against the window.

It took him awhile to find her name and then the elevator. She was on the fifth floor, but he got off on the sixth by mistake and then had to walk down concrete stairs where great chunks of dust were rolled against the risers.

"G. Hansen."

He rang the bell and heard her come immediately to the door. He waited a moment. "It's me, Fletcher."

She opened the door on the chain and peered through a crack. There was the sound of television in the background. Her hair was rolled on pink rubber rollers and she was wearing a pink cotton robe with plastic-looking lace on the collar and dime-store leather houseshoes. There was a stark space of brown ankle between the slippers and the robe.

"Hi, Fletcher, it *is* you."

"None other."

She smiled and closed the door again to unlatch the chain.

He sat on the plastic couch in front of the television set and looked around while she boiled water in the tiny kitchen alcove. It was a rented furnished apartment with plastic-topped tables and fat shiny ceramic lamps and bare walls. It was neat, anonymous and impersonal except for an ivy plant on the window sill and a big stuffed black-and-white panda doll she might have won at a fair sitting on the cheap Danish chair that matched the sofa. Its head and button eyes looked toward the television.

She set a coffee mug on the table before him and sat down on the other end of the sofa. Her face looked scrubbed and shiny, and while she was getting the coffee, she had wound a pink scarf around her head to conceal the hair rollers.

"I want you to know you don't look like Aunt Jemima even with a thingamajig around your head," Fletcher said.

She laughed and seemed to relax. "Where's Sunny?" she asked.

"In the hospital. . . . She was pregnant. . . . "

He put sugar from a third coffee mug into his coffee and stirred.

"That's too bad," she said sincerely.

"I hope you don't mind my stopping by," he said, sounding silly to himself. "When you get ready for bed, just shove me out. I just felt like watching TV a minute and I hate to watch TV alone."

"I do too," she said.

They watched the news and there were pictures of a car burning on Fourteenth Street. The shooting at the dairy store wasn't mentioned. Fletcher felt like apologizing to her for all the trouble and violence, for her being afraid to take the bus home after dark, afraid to go to the movies at night by herself.

"There's something wrong," he said.

"What do you mean?"

"There's something awfully wrong with this city." His

voice slurred drunkenly. He felt groggy from the beer and he didn't know what he wanted to say. He wanted to tell her about Sunny, tell her he was worried, that it was going sour, that he wanted to marry her. But he was not a man to confide, never had been. He felt at ease with Gloria, but he was afraid his wanting to confide in her was some sort of condescension, so he said nothing.

During *War of the Worlds* on the late movie he fell asleep. He felt her spread a quilt over him. She smelled clean and talcumy when she bent near him, and though it occurred to him that he should leave, he was asleep nearly before he finished the thought.

The next morning she went out early and came back with eggs and bacon and grits for breakfast. While she was gone he discovered that the apartment was only an efficiency and she had slept on a cot in the dressing room off the bath. When he apologized she insisted it was all right, that she planned to do that when her mother visited because her mother snored.

Fletcher noticed that morning a list of numbers beside the phone. There were only four—the police, the congressman's home and office, and his own.

 IV

Stepping on cracks down the wet sidewalk from the hospital to the avenue, Sunny looks back at a sprawl of gloomy brick enclosures and then flags a cab.

"Listen," she says to the cabbie (Max Lowenstein, it said on the license), "I need to find some place to live. I have the money, I just want you to drive me around. Do you have the time?"

"I got all the time in the world—till six o'clock—long as you got the money," Max Lowenstein said.

"You know that song?" she asked him, settling back in the dusty plastic seats and unbuttoning her raincoat.

"What song?"

"Lefty Frizzell's?"

"No, don't believe I do," he said, writing on his clip board and then pulling away slowly. "I'm a Berlioz man myself."

He looked at her quizzically in the rearview mirror. "Where ya wanna go?"

"East of the Capitol, I guess."

"You gonna live alone?"

"Far as I know."

"Well, if you gonna live alone, it ain't safe," he said. "It ain't safe if you're gonna live with a company of marines, matter of fact. It ain't safe anywhere in this city. You oughta go home," he said, glancing at her reaction in the rearview mirror.

"This is my home," she told him. "I've lived here forty years. I belong to the DAR, the United Black Front, and the downtown Lions Club. I can't give up connections like that."

"That's true, it ain't every girl got connections like that. You a member of the cabinet, too?"

"Oh, no, I go to the Church of Two Worlds."

"One of them spiritualists?"

"I was Dolly Madison in a previous life."

"That right?" he said. "Look, lady, you sound like some kind of a nut to me, and I'm a hardworking family man. You sure you got money?"

Sunny pulled out a ten dollar bill she'd stuck in her jeans days before and waved it in the rearview mirror when they stopped for a light.

"Excuse me," he said. "I guess there's nuts with money, too."

Max Lowenstein flipped on the radio as he waited for the light. A sing-song voice, bored, impatient . . .

All right, all right. Thank you for calling—this is Ronald Kildale for WXEE. The phone number is 836-1212.

Hello, Helen. Hello there—is this Helen?

Good morning, Mr. Kildale. I just wanted to say that I disagree with that lady who just called in who thought it was wrong to start a vigilante group. I think if the law enforcement officers can't protect us, we have every right under the Constitution to defend ourselves. . . .

Well, now, Helen, do you really think any group which

thinks it is in danger is justified in arming themselves? . . .
Max Lowenstein lowered the volume. "I don't know about
these talk programs," he said. "The nuts are encouraging one
another. Before long we're gonna have shoot-outs on Pennsylvania Avenue." He shook his head. "Nuts are getting nuttier."

He stopped at a light and turned around in the seat, lifting
his baseball cap and smoothing his bald head as he looked at
her. He had a pleasant, even face, and thick sandy hair on his
arms. "You sure you don't wanna go to another part of the
city?"

Sunny nodded.

"I'm not responsible if you live up here, lady, I want to put
it on record that I just carried you where you wanted to go. I
don't want any young girl's life on my conscience. . . ." He
turned the corner and glanced in the rearview mirror. "You
got a big dog?"

She laughed and said no. "But I've lived up here before. I
know."

"Well, I hope you do," he said. . . . "I can't get my wife
or my daughter to stick their noses in this city. I wanted to
come up to the automobile show. Would they come? No. I
say, what's gonna happen to ya in broad daylight? I bet my
wife hasn't been in this city for two years. She says it's dangerous enough in Silver Spring without her risking her life
here. . . . Wouldn't even let her old mother come on the
train to visit cause she'd have to get off in the city. Made her
take the bus to Baltimore. Had to drive clear to Baltimore.
. . . I said, you think there aren't killings going on in Baltimore? I told her, I said, we just don't read the Baltimore
paper, that's the difference."

They passed Floyd's, which looked garish and worn in the
brightness of day, then Fletcher's apartment, and Sunny
directed Max Lowenstein further east.

. . . *people must wake up to the fact that these riots and*

killings and bank robberies aren't random violence, they are
planned, supported, and directed by agents of Hanoi. . . .

Max Lowenstein moaned.

. . . now, now, now, Ronald Kildale broke in.

Max Lowenstein kept circling west whenever Sunny didn't
tell him where to turn. Finally, she insisted he cross Massa-
chusetts Avenue.

"Lady, I wouldn't drive over here after dark, let alone live
here."

They turned a corner only a block away from the avenue
and there was the laundromat with a sign in the window—
"apt." The door was set catty-cornered in the old red-brick two-
story building with large dirty windows, cracked and taped on
either side. Sunny asked Max Lowenstein to pull over and
wait, and he replied that he certainly wouldn't leave her there
if he could help it.

She left the cab and opened the door to the laundromat,
and the heat and the din from the washers and the rumbling
of the dryers spilled out onto the sidewalk. Inside a huge
black woman with a cigarette hanging out of her mouth
pushed a gray mop across a pool of suds running from a machine. In a corner sat a white woman in ankle socks, her pin-
curled head bent over a magazine. A young black woman with
a child holding to her coat talked on the pay phone, and a
white girl in a madras dress folded diapers at a table. The girl
folding diapers looked up and smiled as Sunny entered. She
was an ample, soft-bodied girl with red hair and a wide-faced,
dreamy look.

There were big signs on the walls giving directions for the
washers. One read "ABSOLUTELY NO JUVENILES AL-
LOWED UNLESS ACCOMPANIED BY AN ADULT,"
but there was the thin black boy crouched in a corner, his
knees pulled up under him. When Sunny smiled at him, he
looked away.

"Does anybody know anything about the apartment?" Sunny addressed them all.

The young girl in the madras dress nodded toward the big black woman still mopping. "Flower Thomas will show you. She has the key."

At her name the big woman looked up. She was very black with a round, pretty face. Her face was so incongruous with her enormous body, she looked as though she might have stuck it through a cardboard posing form at a carnival and walked away with it. She leaned the mop against the machine to catch the suds, waddled to the back, unlocked a door, and pulled a key off a nail.

"How ya doing? All right?" she asked Sunny as she passed her. "There's two apartments up there," Flower Thomas said. "That little lady lives up there," she nodded to the girl folding diapers. "The bath is in the hall. Norris, you take this lady up and show her where the apartment is at," she directed.

The boy rose slowly, ambled over and grabbed the key, without looking at Sunny who followed him outdoors and around the corner. There were three concrete steps without rails and a dirty door. The boy moved slowly up the grimy staircase, his oversized shoes nearly slipping off with each step.

"You live around here?" Sunny asked him.

He shook his head.

They passed a door without a lock. Inside was a tiny dark room with a sink and an old toilet.

A few steps away were two doors nearly opposite one another. On one was a sign "God Bless Our Pad." In the other the boy inserted the key.

"Can I help?" she asked seeing him struggling with the lock.

He ignored her and kept turning the key until the door swung open.

The apartment was newly painted green with a silver radiator. There were three windows, one overlooking the littered back alley where an old hackberry tree poked thick branches near the window. The two front windows overlooked the street. She opened one to relieve some of the stuffy paint smell of the room.

"My daddy live here," the boy said.

"He lived here?" she said.

He nodded.

"Did you live here?"

He shook his head and opened the stove door and let it drop. It bounced unsteadily on its hinges.

"Do you think I should live here?" she asked him.

His big eyes appraised her as he opened the refrigerator, which was partially painted yellow. "When they come here to paint, they's a big rat dead. . . ."

"Oh?" she said. "Who's afraid of a big fat rat . . . besides me?" she mumbled. "I don't have to be afraid to say I'm afraid of a rat, do I?" she asked him.

He looked at her curiously.

"What are you afraid of?" she asked.

He turned away self-consciously. "Nothing," he said.

"Tell me your secret, would you?"

He gave her a suspicious look and put both hands on the door handle and leaned back swinging his body.

She leaned out a front window, looking up the street expecting to see a stain there, but there was nothing, only flat, smooth, black asphalt.

"Not too particular, are ya?" Max Lowenstein said, when she told him she was taking the apartment.

"It will be convenient to do my laundry," she said. "And I know the ghost here."

"I'd think ghosts would have more sense," he said.

That night with two green plastic and aluminum lawn chairs and an aluminum cot and a thin mattress from the drugstore, Sunny settled into her apartment. It was strange to her, but she felt she liked it as much as any place could be liked for the first night. It was small enough to control. It was compact and uncluttered, and she would put only very compatible and necessary things in it.

I'm getting down to the basics, my dear, she said to herself.

In the darkness by the window watching the traffic coming and going from the laundromat, black people with their white, democratic bundles . . . listening for the first jerks of the washing machines . . . the first tumbles of the dryers. Across the street four black men sit on a rusty glider and two metal chairs watching the cool night like me. Up the block other people, too, on stoops. . . . On the corner the Mt. Zion Holy Baptist Church of Jesus Christ . . . with its white plantation columns . . . waits. . . .

Somewhere a radio plays . . . *You make me feel like a natural woman.* . . .

My head on the window sill, breathing in all the peaceful, sensual, rhythmic excitement of it, loving it . . . loving its ugliness, the testament of abuse on each street and house. All my life I watched raw land sliced by highways, littered with ugliness, garishness, defaced. Now numb to land-beauty . . . only people I feel . . . their stoops . . . rusting chairs . . . their night . . . people with too much life . . . energy . . . joy . . . dreams . . . sadness . . . meanness for day . . . all these people . . . hearing too much . . . seeing too much . . . outside too long . . . all of it . . . a roman candle waiting . . .

In this room I'll decide everything. I'll understand . . . I'll learn how to live . . . learn myself . . . sing and cry . . .

lean on the window . . . like women always . . . watching the world in front of them. . . .

Laughter from men across the street.

I pour myself a drink and lift the glass and toast all you out there in the night . . . all you who lived here with great hopes . . . you who lay down there on the street. . . .

Always the sound of cars passing on the avenue.

Across the street above the trees the sky heals . . . makes you well looking at the sky . . . children stay innocent leaning back in swings . . . lying on the earth, wishing houses were turned upside down to jump over the thresholds. I made pictures with the trees . . . a picture of a man in a tree . . . across from the school. The other children looked, wanting to believe the danger, then afraid . . . he was watching them . . . children squealing, panicking on the school ground. The teacher investigated . . . pearl flower earrings nodding at me . . . yes, yes, yes . . . a man in the tree, watching us. . . .

See, like you, Daddy, like you, making lies, hearts pumping, flags waving. . . .

Lying on the mattress, listening to the sounds across the hall. The girl Sarah. A soft man's voice, a harsh voice with a threat. The baby cries. . . .

I dream of someone climbing in the window from the tree and walking through the room. I wake frightened, my heart pounding, but hear nothing but a rat climbing in a wall. I pull my raincoat over me and go back to sleep.

She opened her eyes and looked at the cracked white ceiling. It was cool and strangely quiet. The crack made an uneven "V" that ran along half the length of the mattress.

How many mornings will I wake and look at the crack? Always?

She turned over and yawned and heard a washing machine jerk to a start. A feeling of morning well-being swept over her. Her dream seemed unreal.

Across the street the four men sat in the identical positions they had been sitting the night before.

When she opened her door, the girl Sarah was waiting in her doorway in a long transparent batiste gown. Her swollen new-mother breasts were visible.

The girl smiled. "Hello," she said. "I'm Sarah, won't you come in and have some coffee?"

Sarah's apartment was like her own except dirty, and the floors were strewn with books. The walls were tacked with psychedelic posters and a picture of Malcolm X and one large blackboard.

Sarah turned on the record player and Janis Joplin began singing "Women Is Losers."

"She's wonderful, isn't she?" Sarah said. "I mean I think it's so important to give it all when you're young like she does. People say she'll lose her voice if she keeps singing like that. But she doesn't give a shit. She just wants to communicate," she said with her soft voice. She walked to the blackboard and wrote in big printed letters "C-O-M-M-U-N-I-C-A-T-E— Word for the Day." "Actually that's the word for the day about once a week, but it's so important, don't you think?"

Sunny said she did think it was important.

Sarah stared at the word. "That's very like 'communist' isn't it?" she said excitedly. "This is a discovery. The first seven letters are the same." She went to the blackboard, erased the C-A-T-E and wrote S-A-T-E. "Eight letters are the same!"

She made instant coffee in two cracked Campbell Soup cups she'd ordered through the mail. She liked nothing more than getting something in the mail, she said. "Lots of times I've been so depressed, and the only thing that kept me alive was knowing I had something coming in the mail. I'm suicide prone," she said and held up her wrists lined with fine, raised scars.

She sat down across from Sunny and leaned on the old wooden table.

"You have lots of books," Sunny said.

"Please help yourself. Danny works in a book store and now and then he liberates books," she smiled. "We used to read a lot but lately we've given it up. We seem to learn more by talking and free association, you know, exploring our subconscious. We bring up a subject and then explore one another's ideas. We come up with some wonderful images. What do you think would be the worst thing to step on?" Sarah asked her.

Sunny thought a minute. "A caterpillar."

"That's good," Sarah smiled. "But it's a frog. A fat frog."

"Yes, you're right," Sunny agreed.

"We've been talking a lot about Siamese twins. That's kind of beautiful, you know. That closeness. Except they don't usually die at once. . . . Lovely sunshine today," she said.

Sunny smiled, thinking she was a child.

"Last night we were talking about primitive rites. Lord Avery, our dear friend, knows a lot about primitive rites. We're going to keep the laundromat for Flower Thomas while she goes to visit her sister. We have lots of ideas about it. Lord Avery wants to make it into a community center. We also thought it might be fun to have sex on top of the machines during the spinning cycle. Lord Avery is interested in ways of bringing modern technology to bear on primitive sexuality. He was a science major. . . . Science is important, don't you think?"

Sunny said she wasn't sure, but the girl continued.

"He thinks that we should be doing research to improve human pleasure. He thinks the government will never feed people but some drug company might come up with some

99

pleasure pill that might at least lessen some of the suffering. He tried to get a research grant from the government. Of course, now he doesn't believe in the government anymore. He even asked for his application back."

Sarah took a drink from her chipped cup and smiled. "He's a brilliant person. He once had this wonderful plan to buy up all the old geiger counters people bought during the uranium craze and transform them into communist-detectors and sell them to the government. He wrote to the government saying what he was going to do, and he got a letter back thanking him and saying they were referring his letter to the FBI." She clapped her hands and laughed gently.

"You're brave to live here alone," Sarah said abruptly. "Aren't you afraid?"

"I don't guess I'm any more afraid here than anywhere. . . . I don't have anything anyone would want. . . ." Her voice died away.

Sarah looked at Sunny with her wide blue eyes. There was a sad washed-out quality about them as though they had lived much longer and seen much more than the rest of her would indicate. "I'm afraid," she said. "Danny and Lord Avery laugh at me, but I'm always afraid. There have been three killings around here. There was a stabbing, a gang stabbing. They followed the kid down the street stabbing him. He'd break away and run and they'd catch him and stab him. We heard it. He died on the steps of the church. . . . Even the cops are afraid. . . . Have you ever been terribly, terribly afraid?" Her face grew grave and troubled.

"I don't know," Sunny said.

"You'd know if you had. I have. It's . . ." she searched for a word, "it's unrational. You get so afraid you can't get over it. It's like having the flu. It lasts and lasts and very slowly wears away. You're sitting in a room, like this, in the morning and suddenly you're afraid. Terribly, horribly afraid. Sometimes I think the only time I'm not afraid is when I'm high. . . . Do you use grass?"

"I have," Sunny said. "I had a bad trip. It sorta scared me off everything. Pot's okay, though, now and then."

"Gee, that's too bad. I had a friend had a bad trip once and never was the same afterwards."

Sunny looked toward the dirty window, thinking of the mirror where she'd looked and seen her mother's face.

They heard the baby stir and both of them went to the laundry basket where the baby lay.

"He's a tiny baby," Sarah said. "Small for six weeks. He only weighed five pounds when he came. It was beautiful having him," she said smiling at the baby and trying to get him to catch her finger with his tiny hand. "It was like some wild trip."

Sarah lifted the baby and rested him against her breast. His blue eyes stared up at her and his fist moved to his mouth. He had very white skin and red hair like the girl.

"We thought he might be black, but he's Danny's. He has a mouth and ears just like Danny's. When we got to be friends with Lord Avery, we thought it important not to have that black-white sex thing between us. . . ."

Sarah opened her batiste gown and moved his mouth to her wide brown nipple. "We named him Narcissus," she said. "Isn't that lovely?"

Sunny left the girl nursing her baby. The sun made a cape around her shoulders and a mantle over her hair.

It was only six blocks to Fletcher's apartment. The wind blew great clouds of elm seeds over the walks and into the gutters. There was the stuttering of an air hammer where workmen were removing streetcar tracks and the groaning of a bulldozer plowing up the old pavement. A group of teenage girls in matching wool blazers stood on a corner giggling in front of two thin old ladies in hats and white gloves, their long thin necks twisted toward the direction of the bus.

Sunny followed the curved path of Fletcher's walk, descended the basement stairs, and pulled the key from beneath a brick. She opened the door, turned on the light, and started, seeing Fletcher's body sprawled across the sofa bed. He lifted his head, stared at her, then raised an arm and blinked at his watch. He socked the pillow and rolled over on his back.

"I thought you'd be at work," she said.

"It's Saturday. I wasn't going in till later."

"Oh."

He sat up bare-chested, the sheets bunched around his waist, and looked at his watch again. "What time is it?" he asked.

"I don't know."

"God, I'm still asleep to be asking you the time." He yawned and pulled a cigarette from the pack on the floor and lighted it, offering her one as an afterthought. She took it, her fingers trembling slightly.

"Excuse me a minute," he said.

He returned wrapped in a short terry cloth robe, his hair still rumpled. He sat beside her on the bed, where they shared a bowl for an ashtray.

"How are you?" he asked.

She stared down at his bare, tanned feet and thought how all feet looked as though they were dying. "I'm fine, I have an apartment."

He flipped on the radio.

> . . . *she looks at me and she holds me tight*
> *and tells me, daddy, everything's all right* . . .

Ray Charles, the sad man, sang.

"Luxury, pool, and flowing wine?" He blew out a long path

of smoke that intersected the stream of sun from the basement window and sent dust motes scurrying through the air.

"Not exactly luxury, but flowing water," she said. "It's not far from here," she couldn't help herself saying, knowing he'd never ask. "I came for some of my things."

This time she felt his eyes, mocking her for her weakness, her inability to say she was moving out, flatly, finally. I'm a marshmallow, she told herself.

"Help yourself," he said. They were quiet and uneasy a moment.

"How's Cap Tidwell, famous congressman?"

"Okay. Threatening to take you off his checking account."

"Really? That would be a thoughtless thing to do."

"I wouldn't say thoughtless."

"Haven't you told him I'm leaving employment opportunities for some needy, underprivileged girl?"

"I tried to explain about your theory of sublime contemplation, but he doesn't always take your philosophic explanations very seriously."

"You don't either, do you?" she asked him, pushing her hair back with her fingers and feeling the self-pity settle over her.

"You need something," he said. "Don't ask me what it is." There was a tone of bitterness in his voice, and for the first time she realized he would be bitter only toward her and not about what had happened.

"Of course, somebody's got to patronize daytime movies," he said.

"That's right. We all do our little bit."

She took a shopping bag from the kitchen and her suitcases from a closet and began loading them with her belongings. He lay propped against the back of the couch with his sunshades on, reading a magazine.

When she finished with her clothes, she held up the giant aspirin jar they'd bought one day because it was so ridiculous.

"I don't think I need all of this unless I commit suicide. Let's split two thousand, five hundred and two thousand, five hundred. Okay?"

"Fine," he said, not looking up.

"You want to count them?"

"I'll trust you," he said.

She poured him a cup full of aspirin and looked toward the window at the shifting circle of brass animals. "Why don't I loan you the wind chime?"

"No, thanks."

"You don't like it?"

"I've never been too big on wind chimes," he said.

"Oh, I didn't know that."

"I don't usually include that in my résumé," he said, turning a page and glancing up a minute.

The wind chime jangled as she pulled it down and untwisted the plastic strings; then she chose to use the pack of cigarettes as an excuse to sit beside him on the bed. She couldn't bear his unresponsiveness. She wanted to touch him, to somehow affect him.

"Are you mad?" she asked.

"Why should I be mad?" he said, lowering the magazine to his lap. He leaned back bracing his head with his hands.

"I don't know. You don't act very glad to see me."

He let his arms fall and closed the magazine.

"Good god, Sunny, you fly in and out like a bird, disappear, and expect me to flap my god damn wings when you land on the window."

She stabbed out her cigarette and lay down beside him on the bed, her arms beneath her. She shivered. "Oh, I know it. It's an awful mess. I know it's my fault. I'm sorry, Fletcher. Please don't hate me yet."

He dropped the magazine on the floor and turned toward her and put his hands on her hair.

"I don't hate you. . . . I'm sorry about what happened. But I don't know why you had to run off. So it was a bad scene. It will repair. It's not us, Sunny. You get what happens mixed up with the people involved."

"It is us," she said. "It's me."

He moved her hair and bent and kissed her neck.

She stood up and took off her jeans and pulled her sweater over her head and stepped out of her panties and stood there before him.

See, I'm ugly, Fletcher. Flat breasts like my mother. Still thick in the waist. Ugly abdomen, the appendix scar on the side, those grooves that mark where babies grow. And look there is mercurochrome still on my thighs, ugly, and I haven't even bathed.

How could you pull me down here beside you and make love to me, tears seeping out my eyes, kissing my neck, loving my body as if it were me. Me, all a mess but hungry.

But we don't say anything. We make love like we always did, only sadder. Oh, Fletcher, stop my mind; it's never right, is it, with my mind working.

We don't speak, we say nothing, only move, the sound in my ear like a sea shell. Too wary for words . . . question marks, rocking here.

Oh, Fletcher . . .

Quiet beside me . . . sad.

"Come back, Sunny."

He wipes a tear from beside my eye.

Later she pretended to be asleep when he rose. She listened to the shower and the buzz of the razor and loved the familiar sound of his movements about the room as he dressed.

I can love little things, familiar things, easy things.

When the door closed, she sat up. The room and the bed were crumpled.

Like me.

The sun had moved above the house so that the basement room was dim.

Her eyes fell to her body and she stared at the mercurochrome, a reminder like a scar. Only it will wash away, but be there in my mind.

She covered herself quickly and gathered her clothes, sorry now.

It's a mistake this. Never in my life have I made a clean break of anything. Not even first to second grade. I cried.

She bathed and tried to write a note. "Dear Fletcher, I got my belongings. Your 2,500 aspirin are in a coffee mug. I'll get in touch later."

The last sentence she erased. "I'm sorry," she wrote instead. "Love, Sunny."

She erased that, too. "Sunny Sun, the Senter of the Univac," she wrote.

Finally she stuffed the whole thing in her pocket and left, leaving nothing.

Danny, the father of Narcissus, was only two-thirds the width of Sarah, with a thin face, gold-rimmed glasses, blonde bushy Mycenaean curls surrounding his head, and a sensitive child's face and hands. His fingernails were bitten down to the point of bleeding. He reminded Sunny of an illustration of the boy Mozart playing the clavier in his nightgown. He was the only son of a wealthy family that once a year sent him a round trip ticket home to Santa Barbara. He used it only with the understanding that he was not to be bothered the rest of the year. Sarah described his father as a publicist who wore green alligator shoes.

Their friend Lord Avery was a lean, petulant-faced black, son of a government worker, who dressed in dashiki and wrote poetry about the revolution of the soul. He was hostile to white strangers and especially to those with a strain of southern accent. So Sunny, sensing his hostility, declined to attend the final strategy meeting for the management of Flower Thomas' laundromat, and instead sat talking to Timothy Rose. Timothy Rose was greatly enthusiastic about the World Soul Laundromat and Community Center.

"It is truly significant," he said, "the attitude people take toward washing their clothes. It is a thing one shares with all of humanity. As a matter of fact, I might even write a song for the occasion. . . . What is a shame, perhaps, about cleaning clothes is that it has lost its social value. Once the women on the shores of the Nile engaged in their daily socializing as they scrubbed their clothes in the common water. Perhaps the baby Moses would not have survived had his mother not been washing her clothes and thought of floating the child through the bulrushes down to the daughter of the Pharaoh. One could say it has influenced the whole of western Christianity. Of course, it is with protestantism that the cleansing of one's clothes has become private and not quite a respectable public and social habit. I can see the women retreating from the Tiber with their baskets the moment Luther's hammer was lowered."

Sunny laughed and Timothy Rose looked at her appreciatively. Across the hall Lord Avery was talking about the music for the World Soul Laundromat opening.

"Maybe you should offer your song," Sunny suggested.

They crossed the hall and entered the room where Lord Avery was pacing the floor while Danny sat cross-legged on a mattress making notes on the dust cover of a record. The baby Narcissus, naked except for some blue beads, lay beside him kicking his feet contentedly.

"The World Soul Laundromat is a splendid idea," Timothy Rose announced. "I was just discussing with Sunny how sad it is that washing one's clothes has lost its social value. After all, it was done in Biblical times and in many areas is still done. Of course the puritanism in this country prevented this. Now with laundromats and the decline in the calvinistic approach, this social dimension might be reëstablished, and of course it would be especially possible in this area where there are lots of black people who naturally possess a more significant social sense than the white race."

Lord Avery smiled and Sarah applauded from the kitchen where she was painting the World Soul Laundromat sign.

"Father Rose writes wonderful songs, and he was thinking of composing one for the opening of the laundromat. . . ."

Timothy Rose took the guitar from the corner. Sarah pushed a chair in from the kitchen and he sat down. Sitting there in his dirty clerical garb, he nodded to them as though he were a conductor nodding to his orchestra. "A love song," he announced.

> *A poet died far away* . . .
> *In a dark room all alone* . . .
> *Except for a roach in his worn-out shoe*
> *And a flower in his hand.*
>
> *And little children came* . . .
> *In sad, low rows to see* . . .
> *His body turned golden jello in death*
> *And guarded by a dove.*
>
> *When they looked on his golden corpse* . . .
> *A question would appear* . . .
> *The answer they sought their whole lives thru*
> *And that was the poet's last poem.*

They were all quiet a moment.

"Oh, that was beautiful," Sarah said. "Please do one for the World Soul Laundromat opening," she begged.

"Yes, do," Danny said.

Timothy Rose looked to Lord Avery.

"Why not, man?" he said. "It'd be wild."

They returned to her apartment where Timothy Rose poured himself a stiff drink from the bottle of gin he'd brought with him, then continued his ruminations on white puritanism, social and sexual frigidity, and the glorification of the false and the search for the holy grail amidst the mirages of commercialism. "The black people have no idea how we need them," he said. "Perhaps it's good they don't know, they'd never have anything to do with us. If we're wise we'll use our money to buy them into our culture. Otherwise we'll work ourselves to death, destroy our sexuality, and surely all go mad."

Sunny was looking out the window at the boy Norris who with his sheaf of handbills was sitting on the curb talking to another boy. It was the first time she'd seen him talk to another child, though she had noticed that he often sat across the street looking up at her window.

"Sometimes I wonder why you talk to me," she said sighing and turning to Timothy Rose.

His thick eyebrows slid upward and his puffy face looked startled. Then he smiled as though there were a secret involved.

"I never respond properly," she said. "It looks like you'd be bored." She looked out the window again, bored herself by all his words.

"It's simple," he said. "I have a word habit." He leaned back and rubbed his eyes. They looked tired and red-rimmed and he spoke through a leisurely yawn. "I have a word habit," he repeated. "It comes with the faith. We all sit mumbling our ritual prayers so that our minds can escape the babbling. That is our only hope for reflection, when our infernal mouths are occupied with our pabulum, unthinking prayers.

The fathers of the church realized our instinctual flaw from the beginning. The problem is that it is not a satisfactory habit. Its highs are quite unpredictable. I've sometimes thought of switching to drugs. There is an action," he moved his hand to his arm and slowly pushed an imaginary needle in and then pushed a plunger, "and a reaction. . . . I sometimes envy needing something that much. If God were only so demanding . . .

"But then we all love what will have us, don't we? And some of us have to make up a great gray blob in the sky." He laughed as though he found his words extremely funny. Sunny stared at him.

"Do you still love that man?" he asked her abruptly.

She thought for a minute. "Now and then I do. Most times I don't think anybody loves anybody. It's sex or a habit . . . something to lie about because of all the lies we've been told . . . all the dreams we've been led to expect."

"Do you really believe that?"

"I don't know," she said. "Who knows what they believe? All I believe is that hurting children and animals is wrong. That's as much as I can be sure of. . . ."

"There was someone in love with me once," he said. "I was frightened of it. It was not a very happy relationship. But it won't always be like that, I hope. Do you think?" he asked.

She sat on the window ledge and spoke out into the darkness. "I really wouldn't know."

"What a shame," he said, rising to go. "A lovely girl like you. That's the problem now," he said, "nobody will play their role anymore."

He walked to the window to stand beside her and she felt his hand on her shoulder.

"So all those poems are just for English scholars and little children to test their memories and learn iambic pentameter, you think. What a shame."

He laughed suddenly, startling her. She had the feeling that he was laughing at her.

DADDY,

I went to the bank today and they told me you were closing the account. I was surprised but of course I shouldn't have been. I should have expected it. You know as well as I do that I only took your money because I thought it was the least you could do. On down the line a father is supposed to also provide. Provide money, that is. And since money was about all there was offered I thought I'd at least take that. Besides there was money from Mother's house—*her* house, you know. Surely I was due something. But to hell with it. I don't care. Close the damn thing. Money isn't the purpose of life to me, not even the measure of a man's worth or success. So you'll get no tears from me.

I guess that means there's no way now you can touch me, old dad. With that severance, it's severance all the way.

How are you? I hope you're well. Do you still have high blood pressure? I am very well. I have an apartment I like and some new friends and we are engaged in a very worthwhile project. We are opening a community center and laundromat for the benefit of the people who live around us. That may sound crazy to you, but in this area it means a lot for people to have some interesting and colorful place that has some warmth in it where they can come for free. We are very hopeful and think this will be a good thing.

I do not see Fletcher anymore so you can quit worrying about that particular stain on your name. I probably won't even see him again. I think you corrupted him. (I'm just kidding.) Something happened to us. I guess I got scared. And he did seem to change. I don't know. But he is good and I'm sorry it turned out like that. (I think it's because he has double-jointed thumbs. Have you ever noticed? They always bothered me. They look so practical.)

I want you to know that he is very loyal to you. He never says ugly things about you. It's unusual to find a loyal man nowadays, isn't it? He disagrees with you sometimes, of course, and thank God, but not unkindly. (Not like me.) I respect him for that even though I must confess sometimes it made me mad.

~~Of course, he is still somewhat awed by the position —~~

In case you are interested I want you to know, too, that I am feeling very kindly toward you. I am mellowing in my old age. I think of you and wonder how you are and regret we've never been friends since I grew up but were always enemies. I'm not always so bad, you know. Some of the children around here like me. I even get to throw their jump rope sometimes. (You should see how they double-jump rope!) I think of all those bitter things of the past now and then, but I know that there are so many problems, so many things to hurt about right here and now, that I seem foolish worrying about the past. I wish I could forget. For instance, one of the things that bothers me around here is that there aren't enough roller skates. You rarely see a kid with two skates because there are never enough to go around, so they have only one skate apiece. That depresses me so much. I remember how much fun it is to skate. If I were a congressman I'd introduce a bill to buy the kids skates. Or to buy them raincoats and rainshoes. They never have rainclothes. Think how it must be in the winter, sitting in school damp all day. There are so many things like that to worry about. That's why I'm trying to forget the past; but one thing I have to tell you first.

One time Mother and I were in town shopping for Easter and we saw you. You know, we saw you with that woman, Claire. We saw you in the car and she was sitting close to you. Not right up against you but kind of in the middle of the seat. She wore a blue print silk dress. I still remember. You had stopped for a light a car ahead of us in the next lane. I thought I'd die. I thought my heart would stop. I prayed that Mother hadn't seen, but she had. She didn't say anything but her face was granite. I'll never forget that look. It was as though she had turned to stone there beside me without a movement. Her breathing seemed to stop. The next thing she said was, Why don't you get some black patent shoes for that dress. Black patent looks so neat.

Then that time I called your hotel room and she answered.

Please understand, I don't condemn you (I don't condemn anyone but Hitler), it's just that I saw Mother's face.

Please don't hate me for saying this. But I thought you should know. I don't know why I always start off okay and then everything screws up, even letters. It's like a zipper stuck. Are there zippers in the head? I guess so, something like that.

Thank you for leaving enough money in the account so I'll have a few weeks to make some plans. You must admit I've been frugal. I'm making lots of plans here in my new apartment. I'm getting everything all straight and orderly. Who knows, the next time you see me I may be an Eastern Star.

Sunny?

The World Soul Laundromat blossomed. The neighborhood awoke one morning to a Day-glo blue door. The next morning a Day-glo chartreuse wall, then a Day-glo purple wall, then a Day-glo orange one. The broken benches were repaired and reappeared aquamarine overnight. The patrons came to deposit their clothes in the washers and lingered to gawk at the changes taking place. The laundry instructions were adorned with daisies and highly colored magazine clippings. Now they are collages, Sarah said . . . art in the laundromat. The children of the neighborhood wandered in and out delighted with the changes, anxious to be the first to scribble on the fresh walls.

"Scribble!" Lord Avery shouted, catching a child poised with a magic marker. "Scribble, man, scribble!" The child looked at him uncertainly and then lifted his marker. . . . "F . . . " he started.

"Fuck, man, that's been done. Think of something different." He took the marker from the child and wrote: "In each man is good and evil. There are no evil men, only evil acts. . . ." He read the words as he wrote.

"See, think of something new, something you believe, or even something you like the sound of, something that sounds nice to you."

The child thought a minute, grinned happily, turned around and scribbled "fuck a lily."

"Now that," Lord Avery said, nodding toward Sunny and Sarah who'd joined the scene, "does have a ring to it." .

The afternoon of the grand opening, the World Soul Laundromat and Community Center sign was hung in the window above the blue coffee cans planted with petunia seeds. The sign was of extraordinary ingenuity, everyone agreed, the "o" in Soul being an eye with real pasted-on-mink eyelashes.

The entire community, according to the poster in the windows of the laundromat and of the market down the street, was invited to the opening. Colored paper streamers and tinsel were strung across the room, and while the garish neon lights remained, Lord Avery had several pairs of refracting psychedelic glasses to be distributed. Once the glasses were on, the room became a many faceted maze of revolving mirrors and colors. Colored cellophane had been taped over the glass portholes of the washing machines, and the rumble of clothes and splash of suds (some guests brought their laundry) seen through the refracting glasses were like some mad ocean storm where the elements fought with colors against the water.

The opening-night patrons came in their most elaborate and festive garb with beads and floppy bright hats and parts of band uniforms and capes. Sunny and Sarah had made paper hats for the children in the neighborhood who'd been running in and out of the building all day asking how long it would be until the celebration began.

At the door Lord Avery, wearing a red bandana around his neck and a fur vest, collected quarters and dimes for the evening's highlight when all the machines and washers were to be turned on at once. Danny had set up a record player with Lord Avery's favorite jazz numbers—Archie Shepp and Sun-Ra's "Love in Outerspace." There was little dancing due to the nature of the music, so that most of the thirty or more friends sat quietly and perfectly still, listening to the music and passing the odd spectacles, each lens a different color, back and forth along with the half-gallon wine bottles.

Gathered along the outside of the building, peering through the windows and laughing, were the neighborhood children, fascinated by the weird people and the music. Spasmodically they bugalooed on the sidewalk or ventured inside to run up and down the aisle, leaping over legs or banging on the door of the washroom or crawling up in a window to make faces at their friends outside.

Lord Avery and his friends subscribed to the theory that the energy of music should be contained within the body until the body was saturated, and when movement was necessary, when the energy within the body had reached a level where the person must move or die, only then could the music be fully appreciated. It was, Sarah said, a good cheap high.

Sarah, in a floor-length poncho, sat in a corner on a bench beside Narcissus in his laundry-basket bed. Before the opening she had presented Sunny with a green feather boa that Lord Avery had liberated from a local secondhand furniture and junk shop. With this wrapped around her neck, Sunny, fascinated and delighted with the psychedelic glasses, had crawled up in the deep window built for display to watch and listen to the music. When she turned her head in the glasses, the room would glitter and revolve before her, encircling her, and with the shouts and squeals of the children, and the music and the colors, she felt as though she were in some live kaleidoscope of music and sound and warmth and color, all working happily together.

Suddenly the whole glittering scene grew ominously black and she pulled the glasses down to see Timothy Rose who'd added an old, black wide-brimmed hat and his gold cross to his black suit for the occasion. He crawled up into the window and refused to try the refracting glasses.

"With a refracted mind one does not need refracting glasses," he explained firmly. "Besides somebody should watch for the cops who happen to be circling here regularly."

"Isn't it wonderful?" Sunny shouted to him through the noise.

"I thought this was supposed to be a community populist movement, but there are no community people here."

"They were invited," Sunny said. "I guess they were intimidated by all the costumes. Besides, the children are here, they're from the community."

There was a shove and a quick scramble between the two of them as a child pushed past them to crawl into the window. Timothy Rose and Sunny sat back and watched a couple in Indian headbands dancing. They were very young and had very white faces and blond hair and looked very much alike except that one had a beard.

Sunny danced with one black hippy with one gold earring and leather bracelets, but most of the evening she spent in the window with Timothy Rose who'd commandeered a bottle of wine. She felt warm and joyous.

This is the first party I've ever been to where I felt relaxed, she thought. Parties should be for feeling and not talking. I can sit here and not say a word and be happy.

There was a tiny washroom off the laundromat with toilet

facilities, and each time the door opened the smell of marijuana wafted over the room.

"What fools," Timothy Rose muttered glancing outside as a police car passed.

Sunny ignored him and watched some children's refracted bodies imitating the couple in Indian headdress. Two winos stood outside the door watching, and a big white and gold spotted dog had come inside and sprawled on the floor.

It was nearly midnight when Lord Avery climbed up on the big-load washer and began making preparations for the grand washing finale. He made a speech about how technology should be used for man's pleasure rather than man's destruction. He said the World Soul Laundromat was a new concept in bringing technology into the social realm and that he had a great many more exciting plans for the future. Sarah began sticking candles to the backs of the machines and lighting incense. Volunteers were stationed in front of each machine where at a signal from Lord Avery the quarters and dimes would be inserted and the machines started at once.

When the lights were turned out, the room fell into dim candlelight and grew very quiet. Timothy Rose climbed onto a machine.

" 'How shall we sing the Lord's song in a strange land?' " he quoted and began strumming his guitar.

> *The heavens look on us tonight,*
> *The angels peer through the blue door.*
> *A congressman pauses in the cloakroom.*

> *Water is the cleansing of the soul.*
> *Fire is the signal of love.*
> *Death is the only pure beginning.*

>> *Lead me from the unreal to the real,*
>> *Lead me from darkness to light,*
>> *Lead me from death to immortality . . .*

As Timothy Rose sang, the boy Norris, making his first appearance of the evening, moved through the group passing out handbills.

"Mother Myra, Spiritual Healer and Advisor . . ." Sunny read over her refracting glasses.

> *Jesus fed the common multitudes*
> *Jesus healed the sick and blind*
> *Jesus walks along Fourteenth street.*
>
> *May all the saints and all the prophets*
> *Intervene in our behalf*
> *Listen to our exhortation.*
>
> > *Lead me from the unreal to the real*
> > *Lead me from darkness to light*
> > *Lead me from death to immortality . . .*
>
> *Only the violets are gentle,*
> *Only the sunshine is warm,*
> *Only the trees are peaceful.*
>
> *Lord send us a wishing jewel.*
> *Lord send us a miracle,*
> *Lord bless our painted door.*
>
> > *Lead me from the unreal to the real,*
> > *Lead me from darkness to light,*
> > *Lead me from death to immortality.*

People stood at attention, poised to inject the coins, some of them touching the slots so they'd not have to remove their refracting glasses. The room in the dim light seemed even more beautiful to Sunny. There was a vague, misty veil over the refracted objects as though the room were a painting done by Monet. So fascinated was she by the scene she felt the sweat roll down the side of her face before she realized how hot the room had become.

Lord Avery climbed on top of a machine. Sweat stood on

his face and ran down between the tufts of hair on his chest. He raised his fist in a salute, and the pushing and sliding of the levers began, and one by one the machines jerked unevenly to a start. There was a bit of applause from the onlookers and then a quiet expectation at the sound of water gushing, and behind that, to give texture, Sarah had explained, came the roar of the dryers.

The operators of the machines sat back on the floor and leaned against the walls, passing the psychedelic glasses, and to the whoosh of the washers and the tumbling roar of the dryers was added an African drum record which rose slowly to full volume and remained so, nearly deafening with the machines.

Sunny shifted her position, her legs sticky with sweat. The room grew increasingly hot and smoky.

One thin, small, white girl in a long Indian cloth dress rose and began dancing alone in the narrow aisle around the machines. Her arms waved above her head, her long hair swayed from side to side, her face was a mask of tranquility. Watching her, a boy in a black cape began to rock cross-legged on the floor. After a while the girl seemed to grow faint, her face troubled, and she sank to the floor where she lay undisturbed.

Sunny was staring at the girl when Timothy Rose began pulling her toward the door. She followed him without protest, handing her glasses to someone else as she left, and once outside felt a great relief to be out of the smell and the heat.

"The cops will be here soon," he said. "I have a sixth sense about them. . . ."

They went upstairs to her apartment, carrying a bottle of wine, and sat by the window listening to the sounds below. Timothy Rose mopped his head with a wadded colored handkerchief and Sunny leaned out the window. There were more than the usual number of stoop-sitters gathered to watch the

World Soul Laundromat, including a group of young black teenagers shifting on the corner laughing at the activities.

"Now why wouldn't they come to the opening?" Sunny asked.

"They live in another world," Timothy Rose said. "They're as afraid to leave it as we were to leave ours."

Sunny stroked the green feather boa. It was cool and soft and she wound one end around her head like a garland.

The Police came in a squad like an invading army, their red lights flashing as they turned the corner. The teenage boys on the corner swaggered away, laughing over their shoulders, while the children in front of the laundromat scattered across the street where they stood solemnly, some still in their paper hats, watching.

The police cars lined up in front of the laundromat.

"We should have warned them," Sunny said.

She heard Timothy Rose set the wine bottle down beside his chair. "It wouldn't have done any good," he said. "Unfortunately, they have to learn."

She knelt in the darkness by the window, her teeth pressed against her knuckles. "They won't unlock the door," she reported to him.

One of the policemen kicked the door and the glass shattered. From inside there was a girl's shrill scream that died out slowly as though she'd thrown herself off a high building. The blue figures went inside and two paddy wagons turned the corner and cruised up the block and stopped in the street. Slowly the guests of the World Soul Laundromat and Community Center grand opening celebration were loaded into the paddy wagons, some of them staggering, still wearing their refracting glasses. The boy in the Indian headband, shoved by a cop, lost his glasses and, the policeman leading him, moved around to crunch the glasses beneath his heel.

The thin young girl with the long hair who'd danced was

nearly carried to the wagon by two policemen, one holding each arm. She had been cut by the shattered door and blood streamed down the side of her face. They lifted her limp sobbing body inside the wagon and bolted the door, and opened the doors to the second wagon.

Sunny watched as Sarah and Danny carrying the baby basket between them walked calmly to the paddy wagon, Sarah as though her softness would absorb all shock and disappointment. They were like two gentle people outside of time who might have existed anywhere. They made her think of all the people in the world who for some reason could be separated and taken away.

Lord Avery too was escorted by a cop on either side, an arm twisted behind him, his mouth muttering epithets as he was shoved along.

Sunny watched until they were all gone and there was nothing left but the scattered glass and the people watching from a distance hidden by the night. She turned away and lay down on the aluminum cot, feeling a grief that made her body weary.

"Poor Sarah," she said. "I wonder what will happen to her."

"She'll survive," Timothy Rose said. "Sarahs survive."

"We should have stayed," she said. "We should have at least warned them. . . . I always watch," she said, feeling contempt for herself lying there safe. "I just watch from some safe distance. I never do anything but watch and talk to myself."

"What could you do?" he said.

"Something," she said. "*You* could do something," she accused. "You're a priest, doesn't that mean something?"

Timothy Rose stood and walked the length of the room. He removed the big black hat he'd been wearing and held it in his hands turning the brim.

"I'm not really," he said.

121

"What do you mean?" she asked, only half-interested.

"I'm not really a priest. I was never ordained."

He confessed it as though he were admitting the gravest of sins.

"What difference does that make?" Sunny asked, more gently.

"It means that I was never one of the Lord's anointed." His voice was contemptuous. "I was never recognized by the church. It means that I have lived a lie. I was never a part. I was a reject. I have lived a lie to mock them, to defile the role. Only I love the role," he said.

He sat back down holding the hat. His head hung dejectedly.

Sunny sat up and put her hand over his.

"I'm sorry," she said. "I didn't understand."

A soft warm breeze came in through the window and pushed at the wind chime, sending a delicate golden peal over the room. The sound was sad and lonely and innocent, floating over the broken glass and the disappointment they felt.

"Maybe it's good you found a role, though," she said. "That's more than a lot of people ever find. . . . A woman is presented with vague promises of happiness. So she wanders around bumping into people saying, Is it you? Is it marriage? Is it children? Is it these objects ladies make down payments on? What is it?"

She shook her head waiting for him to answer her, but for the first time he was quiet, still sitting holding the big black hat, his chin down, the big gold cross resting against the rise of his belly.

She lay back on the cot. "But I still don't understand why the World Soul Laundromat couldn't work. It was such a good idea."

With some effort he stirred himself. He put the big, black hat on his head and adjusted it carefully. "My dear," he said, a bit impatiently, "one must follow the gray guidelines of the past. Once you vary from that you're in trouble. It never fails."

Slowly he raised the wine bottle and took a long gulping drink and then wiped his mouth with the back of his hand, sighing deeply.

Sunny felt a panicky impulse to rush to the window and scream and fling her body outside onto the sidewalk where she could roll in the broken glass.

"I wish I'd stayed," she said. "Why didn't I stay?"

It's lonely here now. . . . No music across the hall, no voices, no baby's cries, no Sarah passing in the hall, no Flower Thomas waddling up the stairs, or laughing infectiously below. The laundromat is dirty . . . littered . . . winos sleep on the bright blue benches. In the night the phone rings. . . . Sometimes it stops . . . sometimes it rings on and on and I lie in bed afraid of who's there or not there . . . always afraid . . . alone . . . vulnerable.

I am protecting myself with my imagination. It draws pictures in my mind. If I think of everything that can happen, I will be prepared. Nothing will hurt as much . . . but I know it would be different. Like a word one uses, then all of a sudden one day really understands. Like "violence"; a violation, the violated.

My study guide is the people around, the news on the radio I bought, the discussions in the bank and mainly the white grocer on the avenue. He knows every crime in the city. He is obsessed. He says 'niggers' when they're not around. He has a "Help your local police" sign on his cash register. Outside someone responded on his wall: "D.C. cops sucks." The grocer hires a black butcher crippled with arthritis, but big,

123

ominous if you don't know. A huge old German shepherd lies curled beneath the counter.

Let them try that with me, the grocer says to a middle-aged woman in broad, dirty jeans and men's shoes. . . . I'll take care of 'em; they'll leave my door with some extra weight, I'll guarantee that. . . . His eyes shine. A black woman walks up and he nods conspiratorially to the white woman as he sacks her groceries.

They'd shoot more of 'em, it'd stop 'em, she says, sticking a Lucky Strike in her mouth with her yellow-stained fingers. She counts change from a coin purse that snaps like my grandmother's.

You hear about that little girl raped? he says to me. Lived down there close to you, other side of the church . . . coming home from choir practice . . . right nice-looking little girl. . . .

You know why there's all these bank robberies . . . they're buying guns and stocking them in garages. . . . He turns back to his baseball game on the TV behind him.

Why do I listen to you? I ask, hating the back of his head. You don't even have chew-up wax-people candies.

Why don't you move? he asks me. . . . Why do you live here? Why????

The climate, I say. That block is the highest altitude in the District and Maryland. . . . It's a good question, my awful, wary friend.

But where is not afraid? A bank vault? I'd be afraid in a bank vault. On a farm? I would be afraid alone. In a movie house? I would be afraid. Lunatics about to shoot are everywhere. I buy a chocolate-covered mint for two cents. The grocer thinks I'm mad. I stick it all in my mouth and flatten out the silver wrapper and give it to him like money.

Now that you mention it, I am afraid of everywere . . . everyone. Black men . . . black boys . . . black women.

Black men and boys because I can't judge them. White men know my quality. They know a gentlelady when they see one! I laugh out loud and a child on the street stops eating ice cream and looks at me. You didn't know I was a gentlelady, did you, son, me in my huaraches and green feather boa. Listen here, honey, I was a Kappa, Kappa, Kappa, Kappa, Kappa, do you know what that means? It means I'm a stupid ass, my dear.

You children, I'm afraid of you. Delightful, unruly, touching my hair, holding my hands, pulling my clothes and laughing and talking to me, like I'm not some afraid person at all. And your mothers. They put me on, you know. You're such a sweet, pretty girl, why ain't you married, Sunny? Turn about fair play. Maybe they hate my guts.

I have a radio now to erase some of the quiet of the night. I sleep badly. Early there are transistors passing, pouring out warm soul music, the cars, the sirens, children yelling, ladies calling, men laughing across the street.

But in the night . . . only the rats in the wall, someone working on a car in the street. A car passing. A man walking alone. I turn on the radio not to hear the quiet.

In the park a preacher shouts before a bench of four half-listening men. . . . On the grass a couple watches. . . . The preacher is very tall, very angular, he flails the warm bright air with his long arms. Despite the heat he wears a long brown coat over an old blue suit with a tie. He takes off the coats gradually like a striptease as he preaches. A woman is always with him, every week, tall, like him, thin, a dowdy felt hat with a veil. She wears a coat, sturdy oxford-type shoes. She stands straight as a pole, never moving, a poster around her neck covering the whole front of her body to her knees. The kingdom of God is at hand, it says. Jesus will provide, the preacher shrieks, shaking his Bible at the bench of men. Believe on the Lord Jesus Christ and all these things shall be added unto you. Jesus is coming soon, he shouts. He is hoarse from shouting. The woman doesn't move. The hour of His judgment is come. Behold he cometh with the clouds and every eye shall see him . . . and the wicked shall seek death and shall not find it. . . . The man turns, screeching his words toward the indifferent others scattered about the park . . . toward me as I pass. . . .

It is hot in my room now all day, and at night I sit by the window in the darkness eating my ice cream and listening to the sounds of the street and watching the moon between the full green trees. I want to go outside and sit on the steps and talk with people who pass, but I am afraid.

I remember an old woman who said when movie stars die they go to the moon and on their birthdays you can see their faces there shining down. I look for a face. I will write the spacemen and tell them to be on the lookout for movie stars.

I dream a vague, troubled dream that ends with much noise and terror. Waking slowly I discover the sound is real and the fear, already riddling, consuming me until my body is rigid and my heart pounding. I struggle against it, fearing it will drown out the sound that I both seek and fear. There is a struggle, a scuffling, downstairs a man's groan, pleading, the sound of the benches shoved, a tumbling against the benches, an object . . . solid . . . again thrown against a machine, voices, difficult to hear, incoherent. There are curses, blows, laughs, a strange scraping sound, mumbles from the old voice, and all the while fear builds in me.

Someone is being killed! Someone killed! Dying! They could come here! Break down the door! Break down the door! They could come here, in here, in here. . . .

I hold my breath fearing my heart may beat itself dead. If they want they can come in here, break down the door . . . don't think of it! Don't dare think of it . . .

It is quiet. Suddenly a whop, and glass shattering. Another

whop and glass shattering. Then running, across the broken glass, running down the street, quiet except for running feet, running away . . .

I relax, release my hands, clasping the sides of the cot. I lie afraid to move, afraid to turn my head, wanting to close the windows, waiting for sounds, police, sirens, help. Surely someone has phoned the police. Someone, someone, someone across the street, unafraid, someone, do something, something, something.

I can turn my head. Somewhere outside a car roars its engine and squeals around a corner, and I hope, pray it will come, pray it comes here, here, here. I listen, straining, as the engine dies away.

Someone is down there dying. Someone is lying on the linoleum floor dying. I see him lying there gray and bleeding, dying on the floor below me, dying on the floor of the World Soul Laundromat.

What am I doing here, what am I doing here, I ask myself again and again. Someone dying downstairs and you lie here afraid. It is madness, madness, no rules, no protection, nothing to learn here but fear and danger and dying and dying and dying and cruelty . . .

I listen for some sound from downstairs, someone to move, someone to come, call out, cry, moan, plead, even the phone, some sound. Down the street a car stops. I listen to the strains of the engine as it parks, and then a door slams and footsteps recede. I should call out. Run to the window, call for help. Someone is dying, somone is downstairs dying. He'll come, call the police, people will come, will stand outside, turn on lights, we'll be safe, I'll be safe, tomorrow it will be over, the man won't die, only injured, only beaten, how many people are beaten . . . in armies, in pool rooms and bars, all the time, it's a comedy routine, action relief in movies . . . eyes blackened, jaws broken, bruised, eyes swollen, it's simply a matter of a T-bone steak on the eye, my dear. . . . A broken rib, nothing serious, a kick in the kidney, a blow in the groin . . . don't go on . . .

Time passes, the faucet leaks, drips like a clock, reminding me. . . . A breeze plays at the wind chime. I doze perhaps, though the footsteps a long way off wake me and I listen to them, slow and plodding. They stop in front, outside the laundromat. The glass crunches, a small shattering of glass falls, like an afterthought. . . .

A groan, a groan, a voice, mumbling, shoving a bench, quiet, water running in the back, a moan. I look to the window where the streetlight seems brighter now and I sit up listening for the sounds below. I feel the coarseness of the muslin against my hands and then the cool of the linoleum under my feet as I move to the window, afraid of light, afraid to be seen, afraid of the crawling things that cross the floor at night and scatter like pool balls when the lights come on.

I pull the window down in the back and rush to the front, leaving only a crack so that I may peer out. They emerge, two old figures, staggering like men leaving wars in old movies, the one with his arm around the other, barely moving his legs, the other weaving under the load, and the two of them propping themselves against the battered Pontiac on the corner, staggering quietly, stumbling on the curbs, across the street, and before they disappear down into the darkness, I want to reach out and set them upright like paper dolls gone askew. My hand moves out toward the figures and hits the glass on the window, and old and crisp, it breaks. I feel a splinter of glass in my hand.

In bed I light a cigarette and lie wrapping the sheet tightly around me wondering why I am trembling so. I shiver in the stuffy room and finally begin to cry, not understanding, the residue of fear still there, trying to cry quietly, afraid I'll miss a sound. ✒

V

Summer settled itself over the city like a hen settling over its nest, first scratching about and shaking its feathers, and then descending, cutting off fresh air and clear skies, and bringing a smothering, nearly suffocating warmth. Sunny had saved one of the coffee cans Sarah had planted with petunia seeds and placed it on her window sill where it was now a small green plant with one bud. Across the street pots of geraniums appeared on a stoop, and school having ended, children played in the streets all day and discussed their chances of going to a settlement house camp. In the afternoon the girls jumped rope on the corner and the sounds of their chants floated through the windows of Sunny's apartment.

> *Cin-der-ella, dressed in yell-er,*
> *Went up-stairs to see her fell-er,*
> *How man-y kisses did she get? . . .*

Sunny remembered jumping rope to the same words years before and many miles away.

One morning she woke to hear Flower Thomas returned from vacation and loudly lamenting the destruction of the laundromat. Her voice ripped out of her mighty frame and soared pungently up and down the block. "Lord amercy, let me get my hands on the bastards that done this," she exclaimed. "Lord amercy, what in the world's going on!"

Sunny ran downstairs to greet her.

"Lord amercy, would you look at this mess," she said to Sunny as she stalked back and forth in front of the broken windows and litter. A few neighbors and a passing mailman gathered. "Would you look at this mess!" she said to them.

"Norris, you know about this?" she asked the boy who'd appeared from behind the building.

Norris shook his head solemnly and looked at Sunny.

"The cops broke the door, then people started tearing it up, and the other night someone was beaten up in there," Sunny said.

"Uh, uh, uh," Flower Thomas said, pursing her lips piously like an old silent movie star emoting. "What crazy person's been painting these walls? Hurts my eyes to look at em. Look at this mess! Uh, uh, uh," she said shaking her head.

With some difficulty she climbed through the broken door. "Looks like somebody's got killed in here," she said pointing to a strip of blood on the floor. "Why, I can't even phone," she said, looking toward the ripped-out phone. "They used to just burn the wires, now they rips the whole god damn thing out of the wall. Lord amercy, you'd think there's a million dollars in here. But they don't care . . . just so's they can tear it up, tear it up!"

She moved toward the back and pulled the broom out of the closet and began turning the tables and benches upright and the neighbors and the mailman went on about their business.

"Norris, grab the end of this bench," Flower Thomas directed the boy, who reluctantly followed her orders. Sunny caught one edge of it and began helping Flower Thomas pull the broken equipment into the back yard until there was nothing left to do but sweep and mop.

"How was your vacation?" Sunny asked.

"Somebody done stole my new TV while I's gone," Flower Thomas said. "Uh, uh, uh, I sure works too hard to be giving it away to some no-count bum. Wish I'd a been there, I'd a killed 'em.

"Somebody just cut my back screen and broke the window and walked in pretty as you please and helped hisself to my new TV. Ate some ice cream in my refrigerator and dribbled it on the floor. Just helped hisself!

"Uh, uh, uh, that spanking new TV.

"Just let him come back. I'm keeping a gun under my pillow. I'll blow his brains out. Somebody sticks his head in that back window again, it'll be the last time he sticks it anywheres."

Norris picked up a long streamer of blue crepe paper and tied it around his head and sauntered out the door.

"Did he *ever* go to school?" Sunny asked, suddenly realizing he always seemed to be around.

"No, he don't never go to school," Flower Thomas said. "He's a strange one like his folks. He gets out of it one way or another. He nicks his hair with the scissors and they sends him home for ringworms or he sticks his finger in his mouth till he throws up. He don't never go. I tell him he's gonna be ignorant."

"Where are his folks? He seems to live in the laundromat."

"Most of em's dead. They lived up there where you does till they killed each other. Now he stays with some aunt that's crazy as a loon. Most time he sleeps in here. I can't keep him out. I told him I was gonna have him arrested if he don't stay outta here, but it don't do no good."

131

"You mean somebody was killed up there where I live?" Sunny asked.

Flower Thomas swished the broom across the floor pushing a heavy mound of glass, and then stopped a minute to rest. She wiped her forehead and looked at Sunny.

"Honey, there's been somebody killed everywheres on this earth. Ain't nothing to get excited about. It was before I lived around here. I just heard about it. You know how you hears lots of things and maybe they true and maybe they just talk." She turned her attention to the bent rack on the side of the soft drink machine where the bottles had been smashed and used to break the windows.

A thin black lady with a wrapped swollen ankle came in carrying a cheap overnight case. She wore a scarf around her head and walked unevenly with obvious discomfort. Ignoring the chaos she hobbled to the phone, and before Sunny or Flower Thomas could stop her, she deposited a dime in the slot.

"It ain't working, honey," Flower Thomas called out.

The woman pushed the coin return but nothing happened. "I put my dime in," she said calmly.

"It ain't working, it's done been pulled outta the wall." Flower Thomas lighted a cigarette with a kitchen match and stuck it in the side of her mouth and proceeded to sweep.

The woman hung the receiver back on the tilting frame of the phone and started to leave, then stopped beside Sunny. She had puffy eyelids that made her eyes look droopy, and high prominent cheekbones. Sunny heard a series of glass jars roll to the bottom as the woman turned the overnight case to open it.

"You interested in some good cosmetic products—either of you ladies?" the woman said. "They's some good things here," she said.

"I don't have any money," Sunny said.

The woman held up a pink jar. "Take a smell of this talc," she said, unscrewing the lid and moving it toward Sunny's face.

It had a strong smell of cheap lilac.

"Sorry, but I really couldn't buy anything today," Sunny said.

There were some dainty crocheted doilies thrown in among the bottles.

"Did you do this crochet?" Sunny asked her.

"I sure did," the woman said.

"They're lovely," Sunny said. "My grandmother used to crochet. She tried to teach me once, but I don't remember."

"Guess it'll die out like quilting," the woman said, closing her case. "Just die out. You know they got quilts downtown in a museum."

"These kids nowadays can't keep out of trouble long enough to learn nothing," Flower Thomas said.

The woman latched her overnight case. "I just does this till my papers come through when I'm getting me a government job. Selling products don't make nobody a decent living," she said. She gazed at Sunny with her puffy eyes as though she wanted to prolong the conversation, but Sunny could think of nothing to add. Finally the woman said she'd be seeing them and hobbled away, starting up the block house-to-house selling her products.

"She's been doing that for years," Flower Thomas said. "Sells them products saying she's just doing it till her papers comes through. She musta heard that line in a movie." Flower Thomas laughed so that Sunny couldn't help but join her. She stopped laughing and shook her head. "Things are sure bad, though," she said sorrowfully. "My husband and I come up here cause things was bad down in Virginia. But they bad here now. All over, they bad. You hears me laughing, but I don't mean it. Just look at this mess," she said looking around

133

the room. "Why'd anybody wanna do this? Meanness. It's bad for them kids. Don't learn nothing. Don't have nothing. Don't know nothing but meanness and getting in trouble. It's bad all over, black and white alike. Things is bad."

When Sunny left she ran into a skinny gray striped kitten. It turned to her and meowed weakly. When she reached out to pet it, it arched its back and scampered away. In two steps she caught it and lifted it to her face. Its tiny bones felt fragile as a sand dollar. Its eyes were endless layers of blue.

"You're an awfully common-looking cat for such superior eyes," she addressed him.

When she put him down, the kitten scampered ahead of her and jumped at her ankles playfully, so she lifted it again and carried it up the stairs to her apartment and poured him a saucer of milk. He drank it and licked the saucer, then with his stomach bulging, moved to a streak of sunshine by the window and lay down to wash his face. His motions grew slower and slower until he closed his eyes and slept as the sun warmed him.

I take out my sketch pad and sit by the window. I begin. The rows of houses . . . the brick walls . . . iron fences . . . paper wrappers . . . bottles in the gutters . . . ailing sycamores . . . new oaks with broken branches . . . slashes on the sides. I sketch the old church with the plantation columns . . . the boarded beauty shop . . . the battered Pontiac stripped and abandoned across the street weeks before. I begin carefully, drawing my lines perpendicular, creating the illusion of depth and space, sketching the contours carefully, shading, absorbed in my lines. . . . This rectangular surface before me I am able to control . . . unlike what I see and feel around me.

But there is something wrong. Like always . . . in the

end . . . too much. Too much cluttering . . . confusion
. . . garbage in the street . . . houses strangling one another . . . the sky miniscule.

After a while I tear it up and touch with my finger the tiny
sleeping head of the kitten. He purrs and twitches an ear and
goes back to sleep.

It was 2 A.M. One of the waitresses was sweeping out.
Fletcher was drunk and had spent three dollars playing one
song on the jukebox, but he couldn't remember the name,
only V-3, the punch numbers. It was a very slow and sad song
because he felt immensely slow and sad. He saw the woman
with the broom sidestepping slowly toward him and wondered
if he could maneuver successfully to get out of the booth and
walk the distance to the door. He finished his beer and pushed
himself up waving raggedly toward Floyd at the bar. Once
outside the plastic-leather doors, he felt an urgent need to
relieve himself.

He walked down the street muttering curses through the
night air, and seeing a big hedge beside a fence, decided to
take advantage of the lateness and the darkness.

He left the hedge and continued up the street past the
block to his apartment where it occurred to him that the
streets were amazingly quiet and deserted, and that actually it
was very late and not at all wise to be walking. But immediately as the thought occurred, a sense of alcoholic well-being
and melancholy drama came over him, and he walked on
listening to the sound of his steps, feeling lonely and full of
himself, deserted, and exultantly sad.

He had that day learned Sunny's address from a letter she
had sent to Tidwell, and all day while he told himself he
wouldn't go there, he knew that the evening had been nothing but a preparation for his going. He headed east a few

blocks and then north across the avenue and down the street to the corner of the laundromat he'd seen the night the man was shot. He passed, hearing the sound of her wind chime in the window, before he was certain of the address. Not wanting to stand under the streetlight, he turned the corner and stopped beside a big tree with the ground bare and worn beneath it. In a window above the laundromat, the wind chime tinkled gently.

For a long time Fletcher stared at the dirty street and the building and the window with the wind chime. There was a torn sign in the broken window of the laundromat, and the building itself was decrepit and in need of repair.

Sunny, Sunny, Sunny, why are you so crazy, he wondered, feeling a pity for her that she would live in such a dismal, weary place.

He crossed the street to the side door which he assumed was the entrance to her building and pulled a piece of paper out of his pocket and wrote: "May I have the honor of dining with you on Tuesday? Meet me at eight at the Little Italy. I'll be the gentleman with the green carnation. Felix." He dropped the note through the hole in the door where there had once been a mailslot, and turned to see police cruise by slowly in their air-conditioned car.

"How the hell are you gonna hear anybody yell for help?" he muttered toward them and began walking away toward the avenue in the direction of his own apartment.

He passed through one of the new parks that the city was dotting at the end of blocks, calling them vest-pocket parks. They were densely planted with shrubs and flowers and largely useless. Originally intended for mothers with children, they had been in most cases usurped by winos, so that the newer ones didn't even have benches. Meanwhile the children still played ball in the streets.

He had left the park when he heard them coming up the street, a group of five young men, one of them singing, one laughing loudly, too loudly, with a false hilarity. Fletcher glanced toward them as they passed under a streetlight and automatically considered the fact that they were black and they had seen him there alone. As though they'd read his thoughts, one of them called out.

"Hey, whitey, what you doing out after dark?"

Some of them laughed. There followed an ominous silence except for the sound of their self-conscious sauntering and his quickening footsteps. They had turned the corner now and were walking across the narrow street from him, going in the same direction.

"Hey, whitey, we wanna talk to you," the same voice called.

Fletcher ignored them, feeling himself automatically walk faster. They ran across the street and he felt himself afraid and disoriented and he cursed himself for being what was now only half-drunk. He felt an urge to run, but it was too late and he was embarrassed, too, so he gave them recognition with a glance.

They were teenagers, thin, long legged, three of them wearing funny stud hats; one in an uneven beret seemed to be the leader. He wore red pants and a black silk shirt with a silver medallion. It flashed across Fletcher's mind that he was a good looking kid.

"Hey, man, you wanna loan us a dollar?" he said to Fletcher in a sort of phony, effeminate voice. They had formed a semi-circle and were walking alongside and behind him.

"Don't believe I do," Fletcher said trying to make his voice casual.

"Uh, uh," one of them exclaimed with loud disapproval.

Fletcher was surprised at the noise they made and it occurred to him that if they were planning trouble surely they wouldn't make so much racket.

The tallest and most heavy set, who Fletcher thought might make a good tackle in a couple of years, asked him a question.

"What?" Fletcher asked, not understanding him.

"What time you got, whitey?" he repeated. He was embarrassed and annoyed that Fletcher had not understood him.

Fletcher glanced at his watch and said two-thirty, which sent them all into gales of laughter and guffaws. All the time now they were talking among themselves, but he could understand only a word here and there. They might have been speaking a foreign tongue.

"Maybe you got *five* dollars?" a short, very young looking kid asked him.

They were crowding him now, one quiet grinning fellow who hadn't spoken but chewed gum was walking at his right arm and bumping him, and whenever Fletcher turned toward him, he could smell the peppermint of the kid's chewing gum. Fletcher pulled away only to bump against another of them on his left side. He felt his mouth dry with fright.

"Okay, cut it out," Fletcher said.

"The white mother-fucker's gettin' mad," the kid in the red pants mocked, and the others laughed and the small kid danced around slapping his thighs.

"Hey, man, you think this white mother-fucker got anything?"

"You got anything, whitey? You got anything, whitey?" the little short kid danced in front of him halting him and leaning into his face.

"Whitey, whitey, whitey," he chanted as Fletcher tried to get past him.

But they grabbed his arms. Fletcher tried to jerk away and run, wishing he'd run before, but he was swamped and someone jumped on his back, arms around his neck, pulling him back, and quickly all of them at once jumped on him on the ground, pummelling him at the same time, kicking him, and he felt his struggling arms scrape against the sidewalk as one of them was hitting him in the face.

"You goddamn black bastards, you goddamn black bastards . . . " he heard his voice say over and over and over.

Before he closed his eyes, he felt what must have been a heel against the side of his head.

Later he was not certain if he'd been totally unconscious. He thought he remembered someone removing his watch.

He was lying on his back, his eyes half-open when a porch light came on. He heard a lock turn and a metal screen door close and a man in an undershirt and pants bent over him. Fletcher first saw the white hair curling out over the neck of his undershirt.

"You all right?" he asked.

"Yeah, I think so." Fletcher could taste the blood in his mouth and he sat up and spit. Then he felt his back pocket where his billfold had been.

"Looks like you got quite a few cuts there," the man said. "Cops will be here in a minute."

"I don't need cops," Fletcher said.

"My wife phoned. She always does. She sleeps with one ear listening. She's a regular crime-stopper."

Fletcher ran his hand across his forehead and felt pain and his hand came away wet with blood. He tried to pull himself up but floundered a minute before the man took his arm and helped him to his feet.

"You like to come in till the police comes, we'll wash your face. You can't go far like that."

"I live near here," Fletcher said.

He glanced back at the house where the light shone. There were iron bars over the windows even on the second floor. In the shadows from behind the bars a woman's face looked down on him. It was a private fortress. For an instant he wondered what horror had built it.

"You better get those cuts looked at," the man called after him.

Fletcher walked toward his apartment, wanting to run but unable to do more than plod along. With each step he grew more conscious and outraged. He clinched his fists, imagining them sinking into the kids' faces—one by one, feeling their faces give against his knuckles.

He had turned the corner to his own block when the police car came up behind him.

"You the one got roughed up back there?" a white cop called from the window.

"I'm all right," Fletcher said, not pausing, plodding on, afraid to face the policeman. He felt very close to whimpering.

"Wanna go to the hospital and let them check you over?" the policeman called as the car rolled along beside him.

Fletcher walked on. "No." It was all he could get out.

They followed him a minute more then rolled up the window and slowly cruised off.

In the bathroom mirror the cuts were small half circles, probably from a ring and there was already a bruise on his chin. The long cylinders of neon on either side of the mirror gave his face a ghostly look. He rubbed alcohol on the small cuts and held a tissue to his left forehead which was still bleeding. One of his eyes was swelling and his body felt stiff and sore. Fletcher, you are no longer a quarterback, he told himself. His jacket was torn. He threw it on the floor and removed his blood stained shirt and stuffed it in the waste basket and showered, anxious to wash his body of the experience.

In the kitchen he poured a glass of scotch and sat down

drinking slowly. His eyes circled around the dark corners of the room. He could feel the depression settle over him until his limbs felt literally weighted. If he ever saw them again, he thought. The pitiful bastards. If he ran into them one, even two at a time . . .

It was not until he climbed into bed and lay down that the sickness rose in him and he rushed to the bathroom and vomited; tears ran down his face burning on the cuts.

Sunny was dressed and ready to leave before it struck her that the day was her birthday and that Fletcher must have remembered. He was waiting for her at a table in the Little Italy. There was a green carnation on her plate. It was a funny Italian restaurant with all scratchy opera records on the jukebox and a big ugly fountain that never worked. All the waitresses and waiters sang and pinched one another and told the patrons what to order.

He smiled when she came in and like a perfect gentleman pulled out her chair for her.

Just like Rhett Butler, she thought. Here we are Scarlett and Rhett.

Even in the dim light she could see that his face was bruised and cut. There was a deep black-and-blue bruise under one eye and on one side of his face.

"What happened, Fletcher?" she exclaimed.

He recited the events.

"That's terrible," she said. "I'm really sorry."

"Nice neighborhood you live in," he joked.

"It's sad," she said, staring into her drink.

"Of course it's sad," he said, slightly annoyed.

They were quiet until the waitress came for their order and even after she left.

"It was funny in a way," Fletcher said, partly to cover the

silence. "It was what has always been done to them . . . they sorta toyed with me. . . . " He was embarrassed the minute he said it. "Maybe I'll run into them again one of these days," he said to make up. "Maybe I'll run into one or two of them, anyway," he said, feeling even more foolish.

"I guess the congressman had some choice words on the subject." It was all the response she could summon.

My god, she thought, is that all we have in common now!

"That was enough to keep him going for an hour," Fletcher said. "He claims, of course, that things like that don't happen at home. Couldn't! And in his day there'd have been a klansman in the police department to take care of it if it had."

It was the first time Sunny had heard him mention her father with such a tone of derision. She wondered if it was for her benefit.

They ate with uneasy lapses in their conversation. Afterward Fletcher ordered them Strega and lighted the liquor until it warmed. He raised his glass to toast her, but meeting her eyes, he hesitated.

"To many happy birthdays in the future," he said finally and drank.

"The future," she murmured, "has changed."

"Not necessarily," he said meeting her eyes again.

In the car he had a present wrapped in the quick, cheap department store wrapping with the name of the store all over the paper and the package tied with an elastic gold string.

She laughed opening it, loving presents. It was a cluster pearl ring. "That's lovely," she said, slipping it on her finger, but the dome slid to one side. "Funny, I hadn't thought of hands in a long time," she said, looking at the ring next to her ugly, uncared for fingers.

She didn't know how to thank him, so finally she squeezed his arm, but it wasn't right. He had already seen the ring as ill suited and somehow anachronistic. It would have been fitting on some Capitol Hill secretary, but it didn't fit Sunny.

He flipped on the radio.

This is Ronald Kildale, go ahead, please, you're on the air. . . .

Mr. Kildale?

You're on the air, go ahead please.

There was a blip, blip, blip. *Mr. Kildale, I heard on the radio where a bunch of people from different countries were interested in buying the London Bridge that's falling down.*

Yes, I heard something about that. . . .

Well, I just want to know why in the world anybody would want to buy the London Bridge. I mean, why in the world anybody would want to buy an old falling-in bridge and move it across the Atlantic Ocean!

They drove to the Potomac and sat watching the planes and the lights across the water until two men walked by the car and stopped on a nearby bench.

Fletcher turned on the ignition and drove away.

I would like to say to that woman who called in a minute ago that I don't think it's anybody's business if someone wants to buy the London Bridge. If they have the money to buy the London Bridge, well, why not? It's not anybody's business even if they want to buy machine guns for their front yard. This is supposed to be a free country and people can spend their money anyway they want to—whatever the government doesn't take away from you, that is. . . .

Fletcher turned the dial to music. They were driving down Maine Avenue past the seafood wharf where the little stands were bright and festive as carnival booths.

"What are you thinking?" Fletcher asked her.

"Wondering where I'll be next year, I guess. That's what I always think on my birthday."

"God, I won't be in this city," he said.

143

"I don't know," she said, "I'm getting used to it now. Nobody fits here. Maybe that's why I don't mind it so much."

He pulled up in front of the laundromat across from the old battered Pontiac and left the engine going.

"I'm going back," he said. "I've seen this. It's been interesting. I've learned a lot. But I don't want to live here. Life is better back home. There are people I know. There's always a friend around. I like it."

"How can you be sure life is better?"

"It would be better for me," he said. "I know what to expect. I know the possibilities and the limitations."

They were quiet a long time. The motor hummed quietly.

"Sitting beside you I can close my eyes and hear a cricket outside and believe I'm back there. But still there's all this in my mind," she said looking out at the dirty street. "That makes it different."

A siren started and soon fire trucks clanged down the avenue.

"Well, thank you," she said. She looked at him waiting to see if he'd make any move to come in, but he leaned on the steering wheel, staring ahead.

"Thanks for remembering my birthday," she said.

"Anytime," he said.

"Oh, my ring!" She reached back for the package. "Thank you, Fletcher."

He didn't answer.

She left the car without bending down to glance once more inside, slammed the door, and walked away.

The next day Sunny got a birthday card from her father. It was the kind his secretary always bought—frilly, shimmering, saying happy birthday to my daughter with a rhyming verse inside. Enclosed was a letter.

DEAR DAUGHTER,

I'm glad you are all right. I can't help worrying about you living over there in that bad section. I know it's dangerous and for the life of me I can't understand why you'd prefer to live over there. When I was a young man we wanted to live on the good side of the tracks. But then you've always had some unusual ideas.

I'm glad you're thinking about getting a job. I closed the account for your own good. I kept thinking you'd get a job without forcing me to do that. It will be good for you to work. There is something to be said for a structured life. It makes life easier and happier. Sunny, I worry about what will become of you.

Why don't you come in and talk to me? Maybe we can think of something that you might like to do. I'm not suggesting you work on the Hill. I know you'd never lower yourself to do that. But we might think of something else.

I don't know why the good Lord saw fit to give me only one child and I sure don't know why there had to be so much trouble between us. But I'm glad you are feeling more kindly toward me and I hope you'll come in and let us talk.

You know I'm not getting any younger, Sunny. You should remember that. And I worry about what will happen to you. I pray that you will find some man and settle down and marry and have children and a normal life. It's too bad about you and Fletcher, but I'm not surprised. He is a fine young man. He might even have a future in politics if he'd work at it.

I think it was a mistake for you to move to this city and I think the best thing you could do is go back home and finish your degree, maybe get a teaching certificate. I think I could talk to somebody about all those "F's" on your record from when you walked out.

I know your mother and I made lots of mistakes. Maybe I should have let you go to art school that time you wanted to. You know there were lots of good reasons why I didn't think it was a good idea. But I certainly didn't think you would drop out of school and become a bum.

You are a sad grief to me, Sunny.

I hope you will come talk to me soon.

Your father,
CAP TIDWELL

CT/de

P.S. Attached is a check for $25. Get you a nice dress for job hunting.

One evening Sunny opened the door to her apartment to find Norris leaving through the back window. He escaped by shimmying down the hackberry tree. She called after him, at first amazed, and then furious.

The next day she found him sleeping in the laundromat, a sheaf of handbills beside him.

† MOTHER MYRA, SPIRITUAL HEALER AND ADVISOR ★

Mother Myra has the God-given power to heal by prayer. There is no problem she cannot solve. Are you suffering? Are you sick? Do you need help? Do you have bad luck? Bring your problems to Mother Myra and be rid of them tomorrow. Mother Myra has devoted a lifetime to this work. Guarantees to remove evil influence and bad luck. There is no pity for those knowing they are in hard luck and need help and do not come for it—one visit will convince you. Gives lucky days and hands. Lifts you out of sorrow and darkness and starts you on the way to success and happiness. If you suffer from alcoholism and cannot find a cure, don't fail to see this Gifted Woman. You've been chosen through God's mysterious ways

*to come to her for help. Will tell you what you need to know
about friends, enemies or rivals, whether husband, wife or
sweetheart is true or false, how to gain the love you most
desire, control or influence the action of anyone even though
miles away. Open daily and Sundays. A lucky charm given
with each reading.*

"Norris," Sunny said, waking him after reading the handbill. He sat up reluctantly. He wore a striped knit shirt that
was ripped in the back. "Come upstairs with me, will you?"

He rubbed his eyes and pulled the neck of his shirt out
until it caught on his chin. He stared at her a minute uncertainly and then obediently followed Sunny upstairs to her
apartment.

"You want a sandwich?" she asked.

He nodded.

Sunny began making sandwiches for each of them.

"They're having a funeral in the church this afternoon,"
she said, trying to make conversation.

Norris sat on an aluminum chair kicking his feet, his hands
gripping the arms as he stared around him.

"Mother Myra is your aunt?" Sunny asked him.

He looked at her and nodded. "Mother Myra, she have
visions," he said. "She know when people gonna die but she
don't tell 'em," he said.

Sunny handed him his sandwich and they sat on the floor
by the windows and ate, watching people gather for the
funeral. People had been gathering for hours, coming early to
see the body laid out. A panel truck filled with baskets of
flowers and wreaths had arrived earlier.

Norris knew the cars. "Look at that Cougar," he'd say or
"That a Caddy."

After the sandwich Norris seemed more relaxed. He wandered around the room opening the drawers in the kitchen

and spinning the wind chime. He lifted the kitten by the scruff of its neck and held it out the window until Sunny rescued it.

"Cats carries evil," he explained.

He helped himself to some water, sipping from a cheap wine glass and watching the funeral. From the corner of her eye, Sunny saw him toasting himself, moving his lips, making believe with the wine glass. She turned away to watch the widow line up the relatives and then take the arm of the nurse provided for her by the funeral home. The mourners, dressed in their finest and wilting under the noon sun, slowly filed into the church where they were singing.

> *There's a land beyond the river . . .*
> *That they call the sweet forever . . .*
> *And you only reach that shore by faith's decree. . . .*

During the service Norris listened to the radio, turning the dial from station to station. When the choir carried the flowers and wreaths out of the church and formed a corridor for the pall bearers to carry the casket through, Norris rested his head on his hands and watched.

"My Daddy blowed his head off," he said suddenly. "He shot my mama and then he shot hisself right here," he said looking around the room.

"That's horrible," Sunny said. "How old were you?"

He shook his head.

"Do you remember him?"

He nodded, holding the wine glass in front of an eye and looking at her through the glass.

"I remembers him in the box," he said. "I remembers him lying in the box."

"Why did he do that?" Sunny asked.

"I dunno," he said.

The widow came out of the church sobbing, her heavy

body heaving, leaning on the nurse and a young man. They helped her into the limousine and the nurse moved back toward the church, her duty performed.

The cars lined up behind the hearse and began the procession down the street toward the avenue.

"Norris," Sunny said, when he started to leave, "come visit me anytime and listen to the radio. You don't have to come in by the window. I'll be glad to see you."

He scratched his back through the hole in his shirt and looked at her glumly before disappearing out the door.

Timothy Rose stopped by on his way to the mission where he was working and Sunny told him about Norris. "How can he live like that?" she asked. "He doesn't go to school, he isn't bathed or talked to. He lives like a stray dog, sleeping half the time in the laundromat. What becomes of someone like that?"

"Sometimes I think people like you shouldn't live in the city—even people like me," he said. "Our eyes are opened but we have no immunity."

"They prey on one another," she continued. "The other day I came in from the grocery in the afternoon and found a child of about ten cowering in the hall. He was a paper boy. He'd been collecting and the older boys were trying to take his money away from him. I wanted to march out with him and make a speech about bullies, but I was afraid. What do they know about fair play?" Sunny pointed toward the window. "I saw a bum weaving down the street. He wore baggy gray pants and he had that red weathered color they all have. The kids spotted him a block away and started yelling at him. I thought surely he would cross the street or turn around, but he kept coming. The closer he got, the more they hooted and laughed until one of the biggest boys picked up a rock and threw it at his feet. The old bum kind of jumped. And they all roared with laughter and started chunking at his head and body. But he kept going. They were yelling, 'Wino! Bum!' I couldn't hear if he yelled at them, I could just see him staggering by, and when he got even with them, one of the boys picked up a board from inside the iron fence and began trying to spank him as he passed. He landed a couple of blows on his backside, and just as I thought it was all over, one of the younger boys ran from the yard and kicked the old bum in the bottom. And the old man just took it, not even looking back when he'd passed. Later on I wondered what would have happened had he fallen. . . ."

Timothy Rose had been sitting rubbing his forehead with his short fingers as she spoke. "You are a victim of the myth of the noble poor," he said. "Actually the weak prey on the weaker."

He put his hand in a pocket and pulled out a small revolver. "By the way," he said. The gun was black and ominous looking. He laid it in her hands and folded her fingers around it. "Keep this," he said. "Unfortunately, it seems necessary."

"It's not heavy," she said, surprised.

"That's why I chose it," he said.

"You sell guns, too?"

"Sometimes."

She turned the gun, fascinated by it. The handle was black plastic with intricate lines.

"Have you ever shot a pistol?" he asked her.

She shook her head.

"Well, it's Italian," he said. He removed the cylinder and showed her how to insert seven small copper bullets. "There comes a point when it is stupid to have nothing to defend yourself with. In a way you may not only protect yourself but may protect someone else from hurting you, which is also important."

"You sound like the joint chiefs of staff," she said. "I don't think I want it."

"Keep it, I've heard some bad rumors lately."

"It's like a toy," she said. "It doesn't seem real."

"Oh, but it is, my dear," he said. He rested his hand on her arm. "You don't look well, Sunny." The kitten lying in her lap stirred. "You are very thin. You need some sun. Why not go to the beach?" he said. "Get away a day or two. Maybe I'll come with you."

She smiled at his always uncertain and tentative overtures to her. "Thanks," she said, "but I don't want to leave now . . . maybe later." She didn't tell him she had no money. Already she was behind on her rent.

That night she put the gun under her pillow and slept well.

The nights are torturous. I wake sweaty and frightened by nightmares. I dream of wars and fighting and babies lying on the bare ground and people moving over them. I scream, don't walk there! And wave a gun. I wake afraid, and go to the window and watch the strange summer-night processions. People walk the streets now all night . . . men and boys. Sometimes I hear their music or shouts and conversations in my dreams.

The dream of the babies goes on and on, until I write to the hospital:

Dear Dr. Simpson:

I am a graduate student in sociology specializing in sanitary engineering, which I think is an especially good area for a woman, since women have always been closely associated with sanitation, and it is not so likely to engender the hostility of male engineers.

151

I am doing a paper on hospital sanitation, and I wonder if you could give me some information. The staff was very helpful in the normal procedures, but they were hesitant, and I can well understand their feeling, about the procedures as regards the disposal of human anatomical debris. For instance, in the case of an amputation, a miscarriage, etc.

I hope you understand that my research document would not be complete without this information.

Sincerely yours in research,

Everyone talks of guns and being afraid. In the laundromat . . . at the grocery . . . in movie house lobbies . . . on buses. A man is shot a block from Flower Thomas. He sat up, she said. He was dead, sitting on the porch with a hole in his stomach.

At night the sirens ring constant as crickets. Flower Thomas warns me not to go out after dark. You sure better be careful, she says to me, frightening me. After a movie two boys try to steer me up an alley. . . . I run, jump into an occupied cab . . . leaving them laughing in the street. . . . I don't go out at night after that.

Again and again they break into the laundromat, batter the coin boxes in the machines. Flower Thomas curses and shouts in the morning and threatens to quit, but she stays because she is taking numbers now. Every afternoon a cabbie comes by to pick up. He is nice, friendly, open. He makes a phone call. Sam, he says, identifying himself. That's all he says. He listens a second, puts the receiver down. The first number is seven, he says to us. Flower Thomas groans. She keeps a quarter in but always loses. Is four-four-two a cut number, she asks him.

At the supermarket the clerks are robbed and locked in the frozen-food room.

On the radio white surburban housewives call in to talk about rumors of massacres and demand more police and an end to welfare. They are terrified. They are afraid to come to the city.

Bored and penniless children prey on one another, vying over carrying groceries from the supermarket. The bigger boys rob the smaller boys. They all have something to sell. A ring, a watch, a chance on a color TV, candy bars.

Each day, like an old woman afraid her bones may atrophy, I force myself to leave the room, afraid if I don't leave one day I may never go. I leave in daylight, afraid of what I may see. I am safe only here with the kitten and the gun under the pillow.

In my mind I answer all the callers on the Ronald Kildale show. I know them, the regulars, the nasal woman from Silver Spring who reads from right-wing pamphlets. The school teacher with the small children from northwest who tries to be intellectual. The old blind woman who doesn't understand and is afraid, and all the other ladies out there in their house-dresses and bermuda shorts in their air-conditioned houses, afraid behind their louvered shutters.

Yesterday I missed the kitten. It didn't appear. I looked for it, waited for it in the evening. Put its food out by the door. Stray cats ate the food at once and a dog broke the bowl.

I waited on the porch that night and called it quietly. This morning it was not downstairs. I found it later in the day, behind the building in a garbage can, dead.

VI

There was bad trouble downtown. Bad burning, looting, wild, out-of-control trouble. Congress adjourned at noon and Tidwell adjourned immediately thereafter, cursing and outraged, to his farm. There were already a few troops in the area of the Capitol and talk of bringing in more to patrol the city. From the steps of the Capitol the clouds of smoke ballooned in the smoggy air. By mid-afternoon most downtown stores were closed and government offices were closing. Traffic was backed up trying to get out of the city while radios alerted commuters as to which routes were safe.

Fletcher was leaving for good. He had finished his final newsletter and cleaned out his desk. The desk was the only thing he hated to leave. There was something ageless about the desk, the deep mahogany protected by the thick glass. Everything else he could happily never see again; all the marble buildings and the gray slums and the well-groomed houses of the rich, and the chauffeur-driven cars, and the young politicos with their law degrees and unkempt hair. Looking at their smug, solemn faces over the natural shoulders of their Farnsworth-Reed suits always made him want to do something crude and obscene, and at the same time made him love all the earthy, phony Texans who filed through the office daily, smiling shinily at being in the great Capitol City and inviting him to be sure and come see 'em the next time he got to Odessa. They made him love all the people in the world who thought of themselves as living in it, not leading it.

He walked to the window where he could see a leg of the new interstate highway and beyond it a sliver of the Potomac basin where the water was gray and dull as the sky around it. The sun warmed his face and he thought what a fine day it would be on the lake at home, the sky clear, the water blue and calm. He could feel the dry heat soaking his skin, purging him of the cold, bleak, dreary winter, feel the hot car seats as he drove down the highway with an iced-down cooler of beer, the radio blaring, the sky out there in front of him everywhere, open, available. He could see the straight, flat highways going through patchwork towns that looked alike, people on farm porches waving, healthy fields with tractors moving over them, on a hill bois d'arc posts strung with barbed wire leaning as if the ground churned beneath them. The feel of it, flooding over him so appealingly, was so real for a minute he had to close his eyes.

He put on his coat and stopped at Gloria's desk long enough to write "ciao" on her scratch pad, picked up the manila envelope with his souvenir pens and ashtrays and the unused leather address book with his name on it, and left. Somewhere a typewriter tapped steadily. It was a lonely sound. He walked down the empty corridor and took the stairs to avoid running into anyone in the elevator, wanting to leave, to get away, without another word. He nodded to the policeman on the desk and was outside.

My god, it's like getting out of grammar school in May, he thought.

From the steps he could see smoke rising from the northwest and northeast. Burn, you bastard, he muttered and started down the steps lecturing himself as he went. The grapes are sour, Fletcher. So you didn't fit; so you prefer the good old boys and the good old bars you're used to.

But it was more. All that matters is how close you are to the throne, Tidwell had told him once. And he was right as hell. Only those with power and influence or those who wanted it a hell of a lot could be comfortable in Washington and he didn't have that hunger or that birddog devotion that it took to be one of those smug, serious young men. But he had learned a lot. He had spent most of his energy for the past year trying to understand what Tidwell's sweeping political clichés and euphemisms meant, if anything, and then translating them back into soggy, innocuous generalities for the constituents. He had learned that a lot of energy went into making money just like in any other kind of business. Mostly he had learned about the futility of it. God damn, Tidwell had once said to him when Fletcher urged him to support a certain position, I'm just one congressman! Fletcher had looked at him, stunned, as the words played back on his mind . . . just one congressman!

That discussion had tied up a lot of loose ends. He'd understood the uselessness of his own place a lot more clearly after that. He figured he could go back to Texas and raise chickens if he wanted to and never for a minute envy those men with the briefcases who flew back and forth to Washington on weekends.

The traffic was still heavy on Pennsylvania Avenue and the traffic fumes hovered over the street, held by the hot muggy air. It was the last evening he would walk up that street. He wanted to run through the glass-littered vacant lot next to him and throw rocks and shout like a wild man to all those strangling commuters that he was a free man, once more and

forever, soon to be hundreds of miles away from this city of
idiocy and lies and locked cars and cops and troops and
hoodlums and snobs and overpriced beer.

At the corner in front of a bank a young marine chewed
gum and sweated. He looked no more than sixteen and his
blonde country face was unhappy. Fletcher stopped beside
him.

"That loaded?" he asked pointing to the carbine over his
shoulder.

"No, sir," he said.

"Good." Fletcher watched the kid smile. "When you get off
duty come down the block to Floyd's and tell her to give you a
free beer. Friendliest watered down beer in the city," he said.

"Hot damn, that's the only good thing I heard all day," the
kid said.

On down the street past the bookstore, the sandwich shop,
the old CIA building, conspicuous for its lack of windows,
through the swinging doors of Floyd's . . .

We got married in a fever, hotter than a pepper sprout . . .
We been talking 'bout Jackson, ever since the fire went
   out . . .
I'm going to Jackson . . .

Fletcher did a brief shuffle to the bar where Claudine stood.

"I've come to say goodbye," he announced.

"You gettin' out 'fore the niggers get ya, huh Fletcher?" she
said.

"That's right, I'm not ready for revolution."

"I'm gettin' ready to close," she said nervously, "and I tell
you what I'm a gonna do. I'm a gonna get one of them short-
haired marines to bring me over a machine gun, or go to
Alexandria and buy one and set it up right there by the
jukebox and soon as they start coming in the door I'm gonna
mow 'em down. That's what I'm a gonna do."

157

Fletcher tapped the bar in time to the music, feeling her eyes challenging him to respond.

"I didn't know this was the home of the Pennsylvania Avenue KKK," he said. "I knew you didn't cater to the black trade, but . . ."

"This ain't no home for nothing," Claudine said. "I don't care if it's chinamen or spics or little white grandmothers tries to come in here and tear up my place of business, I'm gonna shoot 'em dead."

"That's telling him," some old drunk sitting a couple of stools down said, lifting his beer in a salute to her.

"You're a hard woman," Fletcher said, leaning on the bar nonchalantly and trying to defuse the conversation.

"You're damn right," she said. "I gotta be. In this business and nowadays, I gotta be. I'm a hard woman and I'm glad of it."

"Come here, let me feel how hard ya are," the old drunk said.

Claudine laughed and slapped the old man's arm as she moved around the bar. She pulled a glass from a rack and poured a draft and set it before Fletcher. "Jesus, you ain't really going, are ya, Fletcher?"

"Sure am," he said. "All your fault, too. This place always made me homesick. If it hadn't been for here I'd probably have gotten sophisticated and run for the Senate and been an elder statesman by now."

Claudine laughed and patted his hand.

"Where's Alma?" he asked.

Claudine tilted her head to one side and tightened her mouth in disgust. There was a strip of gray where her hair was parted on the side. "Alma is in love again. She come in here last night with a shiner that I swear'd glow in the dark. I told her, I said, 'Listen here, Alma, we can't have you doing your jig looking like that,' so I give her a couple of nights off. I mean, this may not be the classiest joint in town, but I got some standards," she said.

"Who is he?" Fletcher asked.

"He's some marine kid who's about ten years younger than she is and mean as a mad dog and beats up on everybody in sight soon as he gets a couple of beers under his belt. I had to throw him out the other night," she said. She waved the air with a hand of red fingernails. "That girl's gonna end up somebody killing her one of these days," she said.

The barmaid was swinging her hips and singing along,

> . . . *go on to Jackson* . . .
> *You big talkin' man* . . .

"Course we may all end up killed if this rioting gets over here," Claudine said. "I'm glad it's finally come," she said as though it were an invisible plague. "We've been scared of it for so long, I'm glad it's finally here and we can get it over with."

By god, Fletcher thought, she's scared, really scared. He looked around at the cheap bar with the artificial flowers on the walls, thinking that it was her life.

"When you gonna close?" he asked her.

"Soon as we get the word," she said.

"Get the word?" he asked, but she had moved down the bar.

Fletcher was finished with his beer when she returned. She put her arm around him and walked him to the door.

"You be good, Fletcher, you hear," she said. "You come back to D.C., you be sure and look us up. I imagine I'll be drawing a draft with my last breath."

The carry-out next door was closed and padlocked. The

liquor-store window was boarded. At the gas station and along the streets "Soul Brother" was scrawled on doors and windows. It was nearly dark when he got to Sunny's. A thin gray-faced man and woman sat in the laundromat drinking wine and waiting for their clothes to wash. An old cardboard box with a white towel lapping over the sides sat between them. When he passed whistling they turned slowly like sleep-walkers toward the sound.

Inside the dirty door, there were darker, dirtier stairs and walls and a feeling of emptiness as though the building were deserted. He knocked twice at Sunny's door before he called. He could hear a radio playing very faintly inside until he called and then it was silent.

Her hair hung wet, newly washed, on her shoulders and she wore old jeans that hung on her loosely and a rumpled knit shirt. She came to the door holding a gun.

"My god," he said staring at the gun, "it's Bonnie Parker!" He raised his hands in surrender trying to joke and hide how she'd startled him.

"I'm sorry," she said, opening the door wide for him. "I didn't recognize your voice at first. The radio was going."

He walked inside, looking around the bare walls of the apartment illuminated by one bare, hanging light bulb. From underneath came the sound of the washing machines working stolidly.

"Where'd you get the gun?"

"That priest, Timothy Rose, gave it to me." She carried its black weight to the bed and tucked it under the pillow. "I like it," she said. "We're very friendly. I can understand now why people become so enamored of them. . . . It's like a companion. . . . I mean, it's not like you're alone, you're not just you. You have some kind of appendaged power. . . . It's weird," she said. She smiled. "I'm not sure I could use it though. I drill myself in my mind trying to decide what I should do in a certain situation, but I can never be sure. It's hard to imagine yourself putting a hole in someone."

Her hand moved to her breast as though she were measuring for a hole there above her heart. She looked sick in the dim yellow light, and for some reason he was reminded of the gray-faced couple downstairs doing their washing.

He sat down in one of the aluminum chairs and picked up a book of crossword puzzles on the floor. Whenever I'm really depressed I do crossword puzzles, she'd told him once.

"Can you think of a seven letter word for aid?" she asked.

"I hate crossword puzzles," he said.

"I do too; someone left that in the laundromat," she lied.

She moved into the adjoining kitchen to make drinks, passing a roach that ran diagonally down a wall and into a crack on the floor. Between the two rooms, taped to the wall was a vertical line of photo-booth snapshots of Sunny looking glumly ahead. The walls were bare except for the snapshots, which didn't detract from the impersonality of the room, but rather gave the wall an institutional feel as though they were mug-shots in the anteroom of a police station. He watched her push the refrigerator door to with her hip as she passed carrying two glasses of gin.

"When did you start putting up pictures of yourself?"

She smiled with a tinge of embarrassment. "You won't laugh?"

"I won't laugh," he said.

"Well, I've never believed how I looked. I mean I always looked different in my mind, so I decided I'd force myself to know." She watched him carefully, concerned with his response. "I know it doesn't look very good, but I don't have a lot of visitors," she laughed, knowing there was nothing funny at all in what she'd said. "I remember one time I had a professor who had an eight-by-ten of himself on his desk. It was even inscribed. It reminded me of an imaginary playmate."

161

A squawk-horn sounded outside in the distance, and behind it the sirens rose and fell and multiplied, and they listened until the screech reached a crescendo and began to die away.

"Things are grim," he said.

She nodded, drinking.

"You've heard?"

"It's always grim."

"Yeah, but I don't mean that, I mean something is happening . . . civil disturbance . . . rioting, they call it sometimes . . ."

She stood up and bent over at the waist and wound a green towel around her wet hair like a turban. "Is that why you came?" she asked.

"No."

They were quiet a minute and she realized that she had lost what little knack she'd had for light conversation. One more possibility gone by, she thought. Never a child bride, a movie starlet, Miss America, even a party girl. . . .

"I'm leaving," he said. "I'm going home."

"To stay?"

He nodded. "I'll help Tidwell through the campaign, then I'm through after the election."

She met his eyes a moment and looked away, but not before he saw how surprised she was, and maybe, he thought, even afraid. Her face, he thought sadly, is so readable.

She lifted her glass and held it in a toast. "Good luck," she said and drank thoughtfully, taking large sips of the gin.

The room was like a closet. Fletcher pulled out a handkerchief and wiped his face, wondering how she stood the heat. "Why don't you come with me?" He put his handkerchief back in his pocket as he watched her, thinking her responses seemed very slow. Maybe it's the heat, he thought. Living in this room, in this heat, would slow anyone down.

"Why?" she asked dully.

"I thought it might be a good idea," he said casually. "I thought you might be interested."

Downstairs there was a new sound, a loud hum he decided must be a dryer.

He thought of her reply a minute and got mad. "Why! That's a hell of a way to answer an invitation." He set his glass down on the floor. His voice was too loud and seemed to strike against the bare cracked walls of the apartment.

"Why the hell not?" he said, trying to be calmer. "Why sit in this rat hole? It's dangerous living here alone."

He stood up and walked into the kitchen that looked bare and unused. The glass doors in the old cabinet were broken and a couple of cheap, dirty glasses and plates sat in the sink. There was an old, dirty, revolting smell about the place as though fresh air never entered and the whole place slowly baked day after day from the heat downstairs. My god, he thought, looking out the window at the littered alley and the broken fence, and the overflowing battered garbage cans.

He turned, going back to the other room, and looked at her thin body. "What are you doing, Sunny? How are you living? What do you do every day? Who do you even talk to?" He sat down, leaning toward her, confronting her. "Forget about us if you want to. It doesn't have to have anything to do with us. Just for yourself why don't you come? Even if you don't want to, it would be better. Come sit in the sun awhile. When have you even left this room?" he asked. Suddenly he knew that she hadn't left it in a long time.

"I go to the beach every weekend," she said, running a nail nervously down the seam of her jeans.

"Oh, god," he said.

She held her white fingers to her forehead and hid her eyes. "I've been here a long time," she murmured. "I've been here forever. I don't remember anything else. Everything before this I think I just read somewhere."

Suddenly he felt a strong impersonal fear for her simply as a person, and he thought of picking her up and carrying her bodily from the premises. Instead he picked up his glass and tilted it, watching the ice cubes circle in the glass.

She watched him thoughtfully, seeing his hand unsteady and then got up and removed the towel from her head and combed her hair, twisting it up in back and pinning it. There were soft brown wisps around her face like a child's when she sat back down.

"I don't think I can go, though," she said. "I can't go now anyway. . . ." There were a million reasons why she couldn't leave and a million more why she couldn't go home, but she couldn't think of one to say that would make sense to him. I don't have any money, she might have said to him, any money at all, but he wouldn't have accepted that.

"The petunias haven't bloomed," she said, gesturing toward the window where the buds were now like small closed umbrellas. "That's all the living remains of the World Soul Laundromat and Community Center, and I am obligated to care for them."

She told Fletcher about the World Soul Laundromat and her friends and how it all turned out while he stood by the window staring out and she sat very still on the cot leaning against the wall sadly.

When she finished he said nothing, only flipped on the radio.

Let me give you again the number of the rumor control center, Ronald Kildale was saying. . . .

Fletcher flipped the dial.

Ain't nobody . . . gonna turn me around no more . . .
Ain't nobody . . . gonna turn me around . . .

The sound was pulsating like the night.

Fletcher looked out at the ugly street and felt it was hopeless, that it didn't matter to her what he said or did, that she had moved so far away from him he couldn't touch her. She was like someone playing a strange game with rules he'd never heard of that seemed senseless, maybe even to her, and she didn't even care.

When he spoke it was because he knew it wouldn't matter much any more what he said.

"What happened, Sunny, why didn't you come back?"

He sounded so sad Sunny had an impulse to run and touch him, to put her arms around him there at the window and look out and maybe it might be different, but she was afraid to break the delicate matter-of-factness they had established.

Don't lie, she told herself, even if it doesn't make sense, don't lie.

"I don't know," she said finally.

"Tell me something," he said sounding mad, "there was some reason. . . ."

"I just couldn't go back," she said, "I was trying to look ahead."

He turned, facing her, and she thought he might hit her or touch her, but he only poured them both a drink.

"That's not altogether sensible," he said. "Try again."

"Did you know about the squirrel migration? You know squirrels all over the country moved last year and some of them went mad and danced on the road in front of cars. Isn't that weird?" she said. "Nobody understands it."

He sat down across from her and touched her hand and leaned toward her.

"I'm trying to be honest," she said to him. "I look out this window and try to think, and it seems to me that what I once knew and thought doesn't fit. I am very different. I am different from when I had that baby in me. I am different from when I came here and began looking out that window and trying to really see things and smell things and feel things. I

165

can see that everything else is different around me, but no one admits it. They go on screwing it up so that it all becomes lies."

The words poured out of her in a great burst of energy that had been waiting there for him.

"So I'm sitting here waiting and when I know what I need to know, when I think I can make it with things as they are, I'll jump back on. It will be like jumping on an escalator, a moment of uneasiness and then riding along like a bottle, like all the other people."

She sat back thinking what she'd said, surprised that she had been able to say something she believed was true.

"Look, Sunny," he said, holding her hand. "I don't understand this, all I know is it's a damn dangerous game and the Texas Rangers and Mr. District Attorney are not going to break down the door to save you. . . ."

"That's right," she said calmly. "That's exactly what I mean, there's not anybody in the closet to save me. That's something I've learned."

He dropped her hand and leaned back.

"Sunny, my dear," he said, sounding to her strangely like her father, "You didn't have to come here to learn that. You could've learned that in lots of rooms in lots of places."

"I wonder if you really know what that means," she said. "Besides, what difference does it make? I'm here, this is where I am. . . ."

They looked at one another. In the dim light the gold specks in her eyes were gone. There was no sheen, only a dull brownness that matched the room and the street and everything around it.

He stood up, looking at the line of cheap pictures stuck to the wall, wanting to tear them down and one by one break them into pieces.

"I hate to leave you," he said. It sounded feeble even to him but it was all he could bring himself to say even though he knew that later he'd think of other things.

"I'll be all right," she said. She pulled one of the photo pictures off the wall. It was all gray and black and her face looked flat and thin and anonymous like a woman in a crowd, just some woman standing by, waiting for a bus, caught suddenly and meaninglessly. "Here I am," she said, handing it to him smiling and brushing his hand only for an instant.

He left quickly and she listened to his footsteps and the door downstairs. From the window she watched him walk away, feeling regret, savoring the sight of him until he disappeared down the street into the darkness. Then she poured another drink, feeling a great physical loneliness, wishing she'd touched him, taken his arm, kissed him goodbye. She sat, the pain lapping at her, thinking of all the other things that might have happened, thinking there would never be anyone again to love her.

Sirens lace the night, rising and falling sharply, then escaping, leaving the night quiet and unprotected. I am a stranger in a strange room, a strange country. Voices, loud, boisterous, near hysteria, pass below on the street, the words are unintelligible, only the sounds have meaning. Words spit out, sparkle in the dark, flicker toward violence, splinter the calm; words, curses, obscenities, trampling, turning upside down, frightening everything.

My mind washes, splashes, circles, surges feverishly, sapping my tired spilled body. Fletcher now in a room, filling a brown suitcase on the bed, whistling to himself, moving back and forth, back and forth. His alarm clock will ride loose in the trunk. I am invisible, a ghost, sitting on the bed beside him. I touch where my body lay for long disappearing nights. Fletcher, I say. He doesn't hear. I'm not there, nothing. I begin to cry, the tears roll, iridescent, visible, burning. He doesn't turn to see. He sits thinking of me perhaps. I can't know. Never can I know.

My mind flees. My consciousness fixes itself at some outer point of the galaxy. Around me are millions of stars, bright, brilliant, shining into my eyes like suns. It is too bright for day, making me turn away to night and a glowing diagonal line, an escalator of diamonds. The planets move in a green haze in the distance, moving, circling like a shooting gallery. With a gun I shoot them, but there is no sound and they circle on, over and over, turning and turning and passing again.

I feel a calmness, a serenity, suspended there. A peace comes over me, invading my mind, waving a wand over razor-edged pictures and they are dulled. I think back to my body, and like a zoom lens I return moving into the sphere of the earth, and past the relief of the continents and finally see a speck, lying here still while all the universe moves. I see myself looking out the window into the darkness, caged, moving back and forth, back and forth.

At the zoo a young monkey squeezes through the bars and plays in the trees, returning to his mother inside the cage until he grows and can no longer squeeze through the bars, and then he, too, is caught. They are both captives; the mother unable to communicate his freedom, the young unknowing of his treasure. And so they go on and on, generation after generation squeezing through the bars and returning.

I turn on the cot and feeling cool suddenly pull the sheet over me and realize it is damp with my sweat. But the speck there is comforted, so small, so trapped. Can it hurt much? Does it matter much, that speck there, tiny, so far away, so captured, the fear so foolish?

I drift off to sleep and dream of gunfire and of one long, lonely scream that coils through the streets of the city. I wake, my heart pounding, and the memory of the scream is tucked into the dark side of my mind.

Fletcher was listening to the news reports of sniping in northwest as he packed. He felt a growing sense of urgency to leave, like a child rushing to the swimming pool, afraid he might be the last one in. He was leaving that night even if it was three A.M. by the time he packed. He could drive for several hours before having to stop, and by then Washington would be far behind. He could be in the southern part of Virginia or perhaps even into Tennessee. After some sleep he could drive straight through.

The room looked ugly and cheap when he'd packed. He pushed the hide-a-bed into its couch position for the first time in weeks and wished the next unfortunate bastard who had to sleep on it luck.

He emptied the remainder of scotch into a glass and sat down in the big old chair with the broken Round Rock ashtray. It was a gloomy room, he decided, looking around. The low basement ceiling and the narrow window never let in enough light. It had the slightly dank smell of a basement. He vowed never to live in a basement again. New motel apartments with cactus in the front were better than basements, he decided. He finished the drink and the cigarette, carried out the last suitcase, locked the door, and dropped the key through the landlady's mail slot. At the last minute he'd decided to leave the Round Rock ashtray where it fit in the cut-out arm of the old chair. There was no need for goopy sentimentality to set in yet, he told himself. Surely he wasn't so far gone he had to carry around charms and trinkets.

It was only a few blocks to the freeway from his apartment. He climbed onto the gray, nearly empty new highway and raced past the great hulking giants of glass and concrete apartments in the new southwest. On the right he had a last glimpse of the lighted top of the Capitol. In the dim light, its marble exterior shaded, it seemed warm and a bit mysterious, and he felt a fleeting moment of gratitude for having known it, like seeing a woman you'd once loved, and finding her lovely, forgetting for a moment all but the pleasure of having had her.

But quickly he turned onto the bridge and passed over the Potomac and into Virginia. He passed the scores of new apartment buildings where he'd heard tales of lines of people waiting for elevators each morning, and once downstairs lining up in cars to drive in lines into the city where they worked in lined desks until afternoon when they lined up once again to drive bumper to bumper and wait once more for an elevator.

He drove all the way to Richmond before he felt at all relaxed, with the familiar freedom he usually felt in a car, like the freedom some men feel on a piece of land. He had a feel for the highway beneath him. He could remember highway numbers and roadside restaurants and bars and car mileages and the sound of a good engine. It went with wide spaces and long flat speed-inspiring highways and bright, clean cars. With the sound of the engine and the movement below him he could forget nearly anything. On the other side of Richmond he found a hillbilly radio station and opened the windows wide and put his right arm on the back of the seat beside him and pressed the accelerator down. He drove all the way to Roanoke before he stopped.

This morning my body is old, tired. It moves uneasily. It is too hard to sit up in the heat so I lie here. I turn on the radio to know if there is still a world outside. It is quiet down below.

Snipers! . . . do you think there'll be a massacre . . . . ?
The police are lying about the snipers . . . I heard them.
. . . The niggers are arming. . . . Going to march on the
white sections. . . . The woman's voice rasps. In the background her children cry and shriek.

The old black woman calls and cries. . . .

The ugliness of the ghetto should be burned down . . . a
man says.

I turn the dial, afraid of them all.

All day I wait but Flower Thomas doesn't open the laundromat. Everything is still. The market is closed down the street, its window boarded. The milk truck doesn't come to the white people's house on the corner. Sometimes groups of boys pass but the streets mostly are quiet. Across the street the men aren't on their stoops. In the afternoon buses of troops pass on the avenue, green, old buses, strangely quiet, filled with men in fatigues.

. . . and I said you can't do that and then they hit me, too,
and tried to take my handbag in clear daylight and people
standing around. . . .

Thank you, Mildred, thank you. . . . Ronald Kildale broke
in. *This is the Ronald Kildale show, the number to call again*
is 836–1212. The number again for the rumor control center,
if you hear anybody . . . anybody saying anything that
bothers you, phone 496–0809 and check it out before you go
telling anybody else—all right? All right, let's get on to our
next caller, Gladys of Hyattsville. Is this Gladys of Hyatts-
ville?

Good morning, Mr. Kildale. I wanted to say to that lady
who called in awhile ago that I don't think it's right for
everybody to have guns. I think only some people should have
guns, and I think they should take tests like drivers' license
tests, and know how to shoot them accurately and take care of
them and then they can help, and the police will know which

171

reliable citizens have guns, and call on them for help in an emergency.

Oh, you do, do you? Did you think that up all by yourself, Gladys?

Yes, I did.

You got some neighbor you want to shoot?

Of course not!

Well, who's to keep that nutty neighbor of yours, the one you don't get along with, from taking a shot at you when you pick up your newspaper in the morning?

Mr. Kildale, I'm talking about sensible Christian citizens, registered voters!

All right, Gladys, thank you for your comments. . . . This is Ronald Kildale, we'll be back with you right after this word. . . .

The gun rests cool under the pillow. I go to the window and wait. The sun warms my arm but the sky is gray and hazy. I close my eyes and wait until I hear them . . . four of them . . . turning the corner laughing . . . their pockets bulging with pints of vodka. They saunter as though on holiday, sightseeing. . . . Now and then one or another stops to drink. I lift the gun right below the window ledge just out of sight. I could shoot one, maybe two of them before the others fled. I pick out a tall, loose-limbed boy in green pants who walks with a cocky arrogance and aim the gun at his chest beside the cheap medallion he wears and watch him fall forward, his body curving over, rolling, and sprawling and spilling like a wave. For the first time I see it is possible. . . . Afterwards, how would I feel? Afterwards . . . I could go on living, I decide, yes, of course. I could forget at times. In a movie I could forget maybe. If it were from a distance such as this, I would never have to see the body. I could pull back and not look. But I would . . . I would see the body react like a flawed film . . . like that man. . . .

172

They are closer now and I hear the music from the transistor radio one of them carries. Another of them breaks away to hand a bottle to a man in his door across the street. The man whoops and laughs and thanks the kid as he runs back to his friends, smiling, dancing a little. . . .

The tall boy begins snapping his fingers and rolling his shoulders to the music . . .

I'm a girl watcher, a girl watcher . . .
Watching girls go by . . . my, my, my, my . . .

His arms swing in front of him, and his long legs, rubber, rock back and forth. The others slow their walking. They watch, two of them snapping their fingers, joining with him. The song ends and they walk on, lighter, springier, revived by the sounds they understand and live by, just as I did once . . . all those sentimental sounds and cries uttered for me . . . night radios in dark cars on lonely roads singing about love and loneliness . . . all the things I couldn't say . . .

I pull away from the window and drop the gun into my lap and bury my face in my arms, pressing my cheek against the cold metal of the gun. Afterward would it be hot, or still cold, like now, dead?

Time hangs in a dull gray void. The day does not change until suddenly darkness is there and I am in the night and afraid. There are areas shut off, the radio says, roads impassable.

Across the street a car drives up laden with loot, and children and adults line up to tote the contents inside. The children leap with delight. One car passes with bicycles lashed to the top. After a while the curfew starts and only police pass . . . uniformed men visible under the street lights, both soldiers and police riding together, three cars in tandem like oriental warlords.

At night I hear plate glass breaking on the avenue. It shatters in waves, one after another crashing to the pavement like a great storm breaking. I think of looking for Norris, asking him to stay here. . . . I wish for the telephone in the laundromat. . . . But who would I phone? And there are no lines . . . it is impossible to reach the police, the fire department.

Took me an hour to get a line, a telephone caller tells Ronald Kildale. *It's every man for himself.*

In the morning I can smell the smoke before I open my eyes. The air is heavy and hot as though it were already a very old day, older than twenty-four hours and unrefreshed by night or dew or fresh air. Across the street some of the people pack their cars to leave the city. All day the drunks pass. A white man with an eye patch urinates on the door of the laundromat and nearly falls as he staggers off the corner.

In the afternoon the mailman moves up the street as normal and drops a card through the letter slot downstairs. I race to get it.

"The sun will cure you of all evil spirits. Flee immediately and we will save you. Fletcher."

The card is glossy with a picture of a flat, sprawling long motel and a square in the corner showing a cotton field. Cotton Bowl Motel. I stare at it awhile and want to laugh. It is another world. The Cotton Bowl Motel.

Norris appears in the afternoon and I run downstairs, though afraid in the open outside the building. "Are you all right?" I ask him.

He looks up with sleepy eyes from where he sits on the curb eating a cupcake and drinking a Pepsi from the laundromat where he hides his money. He continues eating, not bothering to talk.

"Why don't you sleep in my apartment now that the laundromat is locked," I urge him, disregarding the fact that he can

174

obviously get in and out of the laundromat at will. He ignores me.

"Where have you been?" I ask him. "Isn't it dangerous for you to be out?"

He wipes his fingers on the legs of his old brown pants and drops the cupcake paper into the street and reaches into his pocket and pulls out a ring. It is a square cut emerald in a diamond setting. The round plastic price tag is still turned inside. I reach for it automatically, wanting to hold it closer, but he pulls back not allowing me to touch it.

"It's beautiful, really beautiful."

A momentary smile pulls at his face.

He drops it into his palm and holds it cupped in his hands like I once held fireflies. His round smooth face is gentle with awe. Then suddenly as if remembering an appointment he puts it back in his pocket and runs away, darting up the street and into an alley without saying goodbye.

I carry the Pepsi bottle to the laundromat and stand it by the locked door. I think it is like my mother and her futile attempts at order and laugh at myself in this city, stacking a bottle.

Back upstairs the smoke seems to be heavier.

In the night she woke to the sound of Timothy Rose calling her.

"Don't turn on the light," he said, "it wouldn't be safe."

"You're breaking curfew," she said locking the door behind him.

"So I am, but they won't touch one of God's anointed going about on his mercy missions. . . . Are you all right?"

They were whispering to one another and she could smell his breath full of alcohol and his body very close to her smelled of musty sweat.

"I'm fine, only a little hungry."

"Hungry! Wait a minute," he said starting toward the door.

"No, don't leave," she begged.

"I won't be long," he said touching her arm.

He was out the door and going down the stairs. She locked the door after him and leaned against it waiting, thinking that he was the only friend she had. It was altogether possible, she thought, that he'd never return and no one would ever look for her or come there again. He would be killed in the street or he might even forget or change his mind. He might come upon someone who asked for his help. She prayed he wouldn't. I need you, I need you, she whispered, please, please, please come back. She began to feel very sorry for herself waiting there alone. She left the door to get a drink. The gin was gone. Only some scotch was left. She poured a glass and let the warmth of it slide down her throat and warm her stomach. Immediately she felt a dizzy nausea rise in her empty stomach and she lay down waiting until it passed before drinking again.

It seemed hours before he returned. Her body was tense from listening. He entered carrying a box of pears and a torn loaf of bread and they sat on the bed and ate and drank the scotch while he told her what he had seen.

"The commercial areas look like they've been bombed," he said. "It looks like a war-torn country. It's bad, all over the city, it's bad. It looks as though it may be destroyed except for the government buildings. There are too many troops around them."

As he talked, she felt an exhilaration about him she had never seen, a sense of usefulness, as though even in this chaos the focusing on his world would be good.

He told her about old people carried out of burning buildings and young people sitting on curbs trying on shoes and drunks crawling into broken liquor stores past rows of twelve year scotch to the dollar wine bottles and winding happily out again, and armed black men in uniforms.

"There are rumors all over—that the president has gone mad, that there are communists coming in from the river, that the south has raised an army, that all the black sections will be razed, that people are being transported to concentration camps, that the wounded blacks aren't being admitted to the hospitals.

"I found a child who'd been shot in the throat. After she'd fallen, someone had stepped on her hand. Two of her fingers were crushed. . . . I carried her to the hospital. They put her in one of the big open wards. There were old people all around . . . people dying . . . She was crying when she died. Her mouth was open. I believe she might have cried for a second after she died. The nurse came after a while and looked at her. 'This one's dead,' she said."

With the night wrapped around them they sat together on the bed, leaning against the wall and one another like two old people who had experienced much of life together. She felt easy with him now and she wondered if it had anything to do with understanding him, and decided it couldn't be that she understood him, that more likely she had simply become more like him, had come to see things more as he did.

"I'm glad you came," she whispered. "I was afraid."

"The gun, you have the gun?"

"Yes, but I'm afraid."

"It's going to be worse. You should leave in the morning. They'll let white people leave."

"You could be killed," she said.

"Yes . . . but it wouldn't be bad to be killed like this. Somehow I wouldn't mind so much. . . . A lot of people may be killed."

She saw him dead, lying in the street, shattered glass under his head, his legs sprawled and twisted. Her body shivered and he put his arm around her.

She told him about the church in Mexico where mummies line underground tunnels beneath the church. "They stand very erect; some of them still have their clothes," she said, "but one horrible thing has happened to all of them—the muscles in their faces have drawn so that each one of them stands with his mouth open as if he's screaming. . . . All those dead bodies lining the walls, each of them screaming silently. . . . That's always terrified me," she said. "It looks as if they saw some unspeakable horror as they died."

"Perhaps they saw God and realized what they were."

"You can't mean that," she said. "You can't *really* mean that."

"Of course, I mean it. I mean it now. I saw it tonight. When the little girl died, it seemed impossible that that was all. I wanted something more so much . . . I cried. They thought I was crazy. I cried. . . . Maybe this hope is enough. . . ."

He shifted anxiously and she felt he was going to leave.

"Will you stay?" she asked him.

"No, I can't," he whispered.

"Please," she said. His arms were around her and she felt him kiss the side of her head the way he would a child, and she knew he would go. She was very little of his life or of anyone's.

"I have to go," he said.

He stroked her head and she wanted to cry and scream and beg him to stay because she was suddenly afraid for him, too. She put her arms around him and pressed her body against his and clung to him feeling helpless and desperate and ashamed. And he comforted her, whispering that there was love and God and peace, and they would all survive.

After a while he left and she lay in the dark fearing that she had felt death on him.

She woke with black greasepaint smeared on her face and arms and lay in the bed a long time dreading the day and the night to come. She would be afraid again and lonely again. The room was still smoky but it seemed eerily quiet outside and she thought perhaps everyone else was dead. Somewhere a dog barked hoarsely but the birds were silent. A loud buzz from a helicopter moved overhead. Now and then a truck moved up the avenue.

Once she heard someone running, that frightened, frantic run that she had learned about, that she knew now and understood. The sound was lonely on the quiet street.

Around noon she ate one of the three remaining pears and wondered if in another section of town people were walking into restaurants and ordering meals as usual.

Black coffee, ham and cheese on rye. Vodka tonic. God, it's hot.

She rose painfully, her body drained of energy. She used her last spoon of coffee and sat down by the window to drink it. The petunia had bloomed. Its purple umbrella was open; its bloom was soft and velvety but marred on one side where it was curled and spotted around the edges. Poor petunia, she whispered to it.

A jeep passed with a mounted machine gun and three soldiers, ripe targets for snipers. They were afraid. One of them pulled nervously on his helmet.

In the afternoon Flower Thomas came down the street walking as fast as her oversized body allowed. She was dressed up more than Sunny had ever seen her and she wore a bouffant wig. She waved to Sunny as soon as she spotted her in the window and Sunny met her outside. Her face was moist with sweat; she wore a technicolor blue dress with a flower basket brooch at the neck. The wig was not large enough to hide all her own hairline on the sides.

"We're leaving," she said. "We're going back to Virginia to stay with relatives till this settles down . . . 'fore we're all killed," she said. "Last night somebody shot up and down the street. I was just sitting in front of the TV and somebody started shootin'. I just rolled out of my chair . . ." she shook her head, "and started praying. I ain't never seen nothing like this. They gonna kill all us colored people or put us in prisons," she said.

She pulled a key out of her white straw pocketbook. It had a dirty string attached to it and Sunny knew it was the key to the laundromat.

"If the owner comes around, will you give him the key?" she asked.

"Sure," Sunny said.

Flower Thomas looked at the broken front of the laundromat. "It don't matter to me if they tears it the rest of the way up," she said, touching her wig. "Uh, uh, uh, it'll take him till Jesus comes to get it repaired anyway. . . ."

She handed the key to Sunny and turned to leave. "You sure better get outta here, too," she called back over her shoulder as she walked away.

Sunny had been asleep when she was wakened by the shouts on the street. It was dusk but light enough so that she could see them in a large ragged group moving up toward the avenue breaking windows as they passed. Across the street several people were peering from behind their shades. Most of the houses had installed Soul Brother signs in the windows or painted them on the house or door.

The group was young, colorfully dressed, excited. They searched for rocks as they moved. Some of them carried sticks, some guns. They circled a blue Mustang down the street and began rocking it. The car shuddered on its springs and finally rolled over and lay like a dead bug with its wheels up. One of the boys stuck a rag in the gas tank, lighted it, and they ran back. It was like kids playing with fire crackers, Sunny thought. The car exploded and burned slowly. Another boy passed around a bottle until it was empty, then smashed it against the windshield of another car. They moved slowly, like an army of children. There were a few girls; one of them wore tall, gold boots and pulled a shopping cart full of clothes and cartons of cigarettes. Another girl wore a great purple hat and carried a lamp over her shoulder.

Sunny crouched beside the window listening as they passed. She heard some of them stop in front of the laundromat and then rocks splatter against the boarded windows. Finally she heard them smash through the boards and enter.

The wind chime moved, playing gently.

"A white mother-fucker lives upstairs."

The words struck her like stones, then a rock came sailing through the window, shattering glass at the top, spraying it over the room and around her. Slowly she crawled to the bed, crouched on the other side and pulled the gun out from under the pillow and piled the copper bullets beside her. The cot was between herself and the door, and she rested her hand on the mattress and pointed the gun toward the door and waited, her heart racing.

Downstairs they were battering a car.

Try to think, she told herself. Hide. Yes, if I could hide. But she was afraid to move.

She might be able to hide in the apartment across the hall, climb onto the roof through a window, but she was afraid to stand, afraid to open the door, cross the hall, afraid to make a sound.

Out the window she heard a siren in the distance. The battering stopped outside and she heard running over the shattering glass and then the siren came nearer as though it were coming down the avenue toward them. She heard the front door open and voices in the hall and on the steps leading upstairs. They were laughing and talking, speaking unintelligibly, senselessly, but her head pounded so that there was no sense to her anywhere.

Think, think, she told herself. If they come up the stairs . . .

The gun quivered in her hands and she wondered for a moment if she might be unable to act, if fear might render her as helpless as one pursued in a dream and unable to move.

If they come up the stairs and try to open the door. They can break it easily. If they break the door and enter the room I'll shoot. . . . They'll shoot. . . . What if they shoot . . . ? I'll hide. I'll say there's nothing here and they'll go away. But they won't go away. I'll shoot before they open the door. Shoot low, shoot someone in the leg, maybe it will miss, maybe just frighten them away. They'll come back, later in the dark. . . . But they are just people, like me, just people.

The siren seemed very near now and loud, it filled her ears. She prayed for it to come nearer. She would rush to the window and scream to it. And then slowly she heard it begin to diminish, and then laughter downstairs in the hall and footsteps on the stairs, slowly, steps coming up. She heard the door across the hall open.

She caught her breath and in a minute she heard him cross to her door. The door handle turned.

It turned the other way. Shook impatiently. Then he moved, turned . . . walked away.

There was a shout from downstairs.

Then, "Hey, man, I'm pissing . . ."

She heard the door downstairs open. A few minutes later footsteps descending the stairs, two at a time, jumping, hurrying, and the door opened again and it was quiet.

She leaned on the mattress, letting the gun fall, and put her head in her arm, praying her heart would calm before it pounded itself dead.

I could die in this room. I could be killed, my body lying here on this worn linoleum, growing cold, colder than its faded shiny surface. No one would know. No one would find me here. They could burn the building and I would disappear. I would be annihilated. No one would know or care and I would be gone, there would be nothing left. I would be nowhere, only my body in this ugly, god-hated room.

My heart is like ice it is so afraid. Fear pounds in my ears. Fear like a thing, a great presence of wind and power that has gripped my body like a hurricane, like all the monsters in the movies, all the horrors in the horror houses, all the ghosts and haunted houses and bombs and wars and guns and prisons . . .

Have you ever been really afraid, Sarah asked.

Yes, yes, yes, yes.

My body has no heat. It is an icy hollowed-out object but there is sweat on my forehead and beneath my arms and a smell about my body which is unfamiliar. It is fear, the smell of fear.

I wait sitting here in the darkness, afraid to move, waiting behind the cot, my fingers touching the gun. I turn the little yellow box upside down and make a pile of gold bullets on the bed. I run them through my fingers, like jewels. . . . They are cool, solid. . . . I am a miser, caressing them. . . .

I wait for someone. The scotch bottle is empty beside the bed. Scotch is the answer. If only I could pour water into the bottle, but I am afraid to move. I hold the empty bottle to my lips but it is useless. I wait.

Some water in the bottle, I tell myself, it would help.

Finally I rise, surprised that nothing happens, and walk quietly making no sound into the kitchen. The pipes shake when I turn the faucet and I close it quickly and wait and then hearing nothing I turn it again until only a trickle runs out and into the bottle and I shake it, turning the bottle so that the water slides across the sides.

I tiptoe slowly back to the cot and sit down and raise the bottle to my lips, but it is only tainted water and disappointing. I want to cry. . . .

I lie, my head on the cot, the butt of the gun touching my head. Exhausted my mind retreats, I am nothing here already . . .

The footsteps grow from inside of me. They grow there till my body and the room and the building are all swallowed by them. They are sad, slow, strange steps, like someone afraid or someone stalking carefully. They reach the top of the stairs and stop in front of my door.

So you are back, my friend. . . . I'll greet you, my friend, you, one I've waited for . . .

I raise the gun and point it toward the door. My hand moves without effort as though my mind turns it. There is a loud knock. Then again and again, an irrational thumping like someone gone mad. The door handle turns. I catch my breath. But I am cool, a vegetable growing here out of this floor. It turns and rattles and it is unbearably quiet a minute. I think of the two of us facing one another, quietly waiting.

"Who is it?" I call. My voice uneven and low like the scraping of a chair across a floor.

Nothing. But he heard. He knows I'm here. Like a ghost, once they know! Once you give in your presence. I'll never be safe. He'll always know. He'll come in now. So it is necessary. I can't be seen, touched, plucked here.

I steady the gun, thinking of the bullets suspended there in the chamber waiting. I am resting the elbows on the bed. The gun is part of the hands, grows out of the arms, and the trigger pulls easily.

The explosion jolts my arm upward and there is smoke in front of me and for a minute I think it is me exploded and dead and I feel nearly peaceful, my ears ringing. But there is a movement outside the door and I pull the trigger again and again, thinking myself numb, a machine exploding.

And then quiet. The gun is barely warm in my hands.

I wait, I stand up slowly, my legs unsteady; and crouching over, afraid to stand straight, I move to the door and run my fingers gently over the holes, pressing my cheek to them like a lover. There is a queer smell in the room like fire crackers, and it is quieter, so quiet I believe my ears are gone, blown away. I lean against the door. My head is dizzy and I clutch the handle for support. There are colors rushing through my mind like fireworks passing through and a thought comes to me. I'm afraid the thought will destroy my mind, end it, cease its function. I clap my hand to my mouth to stop the scream inside me from coming out, and I pull open the door.

A trail of street light runs across the room and out the door diagonally across his body. He wears a new jacket too heavy for the heat. There is a tag still on the back of the sleeve. His thin body is not flat against the ground, not resting, but crumpled and distorted, like a partially crushed paper bag with one arm caught under him, under his dirty brown pants.

I lay the gun down and kneel beside him.

"Norris."

I take his hand and hold it to my face. It is dry and unsmooth and the size of my own.

"Norris."

I want to take his body into mine and rip myself apart and repair his with my cells and blood and breath, all those things that still work when it doesn't matter. I want to take him and the world into my body and rebuild them until I am used up.

I feel my knee damp. A rivulet of blood runs from under his body. I watch it cross on the splintery wooden floor. For a minute it pools at the edge of the landing where the wood is worn down by years and years of footsteps.

 VII

As soon as he reached Texas Fletcher wired Sunny: "Weather good, beer cold, will send money, please come. Love Fletcher."

Then he checked into a motel room, took a shower, turned up the air conditioner to high, had a stiff drink, and slept for fourteen hours. When he woke the cobwebs were gone, the gray smog of the city had been exhaled from his system and expelled by the droning machine in the window. He lay in the darkened cool room against the tight white sheets feeling life seeping back into him. Through the edge of the blinds he could see the stark sun beating down on the gravel drive. He knew just what to expect, what the sun would feel like, how the streets would sound, how the girls' voices would twang and drawl softly, where his friends would be drinking and swapping stories. There was a comfort in what he knew, in knowing what to expect, in knowing he could sit down somewhere and feel as though it was the same as it had been.

He dressed, had a midday breakfast with hash browns and phoned Tidwell.

"Hell, you know I'd be the last to hear from Sunny," Tidwell told him. "Don't worry, boy, she'll turn up like a bad penny, she always does. I tried calling the po-lice about her but they're all going crazy. They wouldn't know if she was hanging from the ceiling down there.

"Ever tell you about the time she flew to Alaska in the middle of the earthquakes to help the Red Cross? She's probably gone to New York. Hell, she may be in Afghanistan. She's been known to consider it."

The conversation was unpleasant and made Fletcher even happier that he was through with Washington and nearly through with Tidwell. When he put down the receiver, he cursed Tidwell as he walked to his car. Once inside he told himself to forget it and by the time he'd pulled out into the traffic he had.

He drove past all the familiar stores and houses and noted the changes—the new buildings, and the new parking meters and the bigger stoplights. He drove—simply drove, up and down the streets like a teenager driving for the fun of driving through familiar territory.

After a while he went to Rio-Rio's and pushed open the door with the old "It's Cool Inside" sign. Rio-Rio was a plump, pretty Mexican woman with a big gold tooth in front who served beer and hot chili and various other mouth-scorching Mexican foods. Inside the door under the picture of the Blessed Virgin Mary stood the new brown bulky body of a cigarette machine.

"That's the end of my business," he called to Rio-Rio behind the cash register where she was lining up chewing gum.

She smiled with her big gold tooth and red gums, her gold-cross earrings dangling from her ears.

He sat at the counter and asked her about her daughter in business school and her two sons in the moving business and how her business was going and if she'd moved into her new house. He told her he was expecting a telegram there and while eating tacos and drinking beer composed another, scribbling it on a napkin. He decided on, "Please phone. Rio-Rio on death bed calls for you. Fletcher."

He phoned in the telegram and charged it to Tidwell's campaign headquarters.

After the tacos he moved to the back booth and tried to work on a speech to a farmers' group. It was an important speech for Tidwell, and one he could use several times in the campaign, but at the moment Fletcher felt as remote from farm problems as from prohibition. He wondered if there was anything he could say about Washington that would be at all relevant to their problems and interests. He could tell them how lucky they were to have clear air and a stretch of open field for their kids to run in. He would have liked to have pointed out to some of those rich farmers who'd been collecting money from the government for not working their land, that had some of that money gone to the people who had once worked the land for them, maybe there wouldn't be so many people crowded into the ghettos of the city. The trouble with talking to farmers now was that they were either very rich or very poor with few in between, and the ones Tidwell talked to mostly were the rich ones and they were as paranoid on the cities as Tidwell.

"Why, Dallas is the only safe city left in the country," one of them told him not long ago. "I wouldn't take my wife anywhere but Dallas. I wouldn't even take her to Houston, she might get shot in the back. In Dallas, they know how to keep law and order."

Fletcher had wanted to kick the son of a bitch in the teeth, but he'd only grimaced and turned away.

Some of the poor farmers he thought he could talk to because they knew about being poor. Listen, he'd liked to have said to them, these people in the cities had to leave the country because they couldn't make a living. Now you all know about that. There's not one of you hasn't thought about it or had some relative that had to do it. That's what *they* did, but most of them being black couldn't get decent jobs because they didn't know anything but farming and they didn't have land to plant a garden. Maybe the best they could do is send their wives out as domestics. So you end up with lots of poor people living close in cheap places. You drive through parts of the cities and you see signs on grocery stores saying "Pig tails fifteen cents a pound." Now you all know what kind of eating pig tails is. It doesn't make for happy, contented evenings.

Fletcher thought of Charlie Daniels. Charlie Daniels and his leather face looking fifty at thirty, spawning kids out of his skinny, bow-legged wife like tadpoles, all of them blonde and skinny and sad-faced just like her. The last time he saw Charlie Daniels he was filling his gas tank and talking about how he hated living in town where it was so noisy. He had laughed. Funny thing, he'd said, is what he missed most was the noise on his farm. He'd never in his life had to live without chickens and livestock serenading him when he stepped outside the house. Charlie Daniels had sold his farm the year he got four cents a pound for his tomatoes and his wife had to have an operation.

The thing to do, Fletcher decided, was to drive out tomorrow and talk to some of the farmers and get some ideas. He had to get back in touch, lean on some fence post awhile and chat with some sandy-land farmer who could tell him what kind of insects were destroying his cotton that year.

He left Rio-Rio's and drove out to the lake where Buddy Pynes was living and found a party. They were cooking hamburgers outside and dancing on the sun deck that looked out over the lake. Sheila, big with child, hugged him warmly and everyone seemed delighted to see him. He walked around drinking beer and telling Washington stories.

There was a new girl, a blonde from Kilgore, barefooted in some skimpy outfit with a bare stomach. She had the clean, clear-skinned face of a rich girl and Buddy verified that her father had made a pile with some new oil rigging equipment. But she's okay, Buddy said. A little young, but broke in.

The party was good, not too big, not too drunken and Fletcher felt good being around friends. The new girl called herself Casey. "I was big for my age in the fifth grade," she said, "so I became a famed slugger. It's better than Cynthia, don't you think?"

He agreed heartily and thought that she felt good in his arms and that she had a sexy way of sticking her bottom out a little when she danced.

She had just returned from Spain and she wasn't doing much of anything, halfway looking for a job, she said. "Granada is like a flower garden," she told him. "You drive down from the mountains and the fragrance meets you outside of town."

In the faint light of the patio her oval eyes against her tan face were luminous and tantalizing.

"You any kin to an Indian?" he asked her.

"How did you know?" she asked. "My grandmother was half Cherokee. She was mean as hell."

"I've always liked Indians," he said.

"And the temper that goes with it?" She smiled and wondered aloud how she'd get back to town.

Later in the car he felt no necessity to talk. They drove silently down the narrow lake road and onto the highway, the night warm and fresh. The highway was built up off the land so that they looked down on farmland with thick cotton fields and rows of corn, and at their sides the sky stretched out all around them.

"You know," he said to her, "I really feel like I'm home and it's damned pleasant. Time even passes differently," he said.

"You sound as though you're home from the wars," she said.

"That's not a bad way to put it. Washington is no playground."

"Were you there when it started?" she asked.

He told her about standing on the steps of the House Office Building and seeing the smoke behind the Capitol.

He put two cigarettes in his mouth and lighted them and handed one to her.

"I decided this summer that I'm just a country girl," she said. "I like to go barefoot and know who's around me and understand where I am. Spain was fun but I didn't understand those people or that country and it would take a long time to learn. I think I want to live where I feel comfortable," she said.

And he thought she understood more than she bothered to say.

They reached the edge of town and passed a new shopping center and the old turkey farm and the automobile graveyard with the hub caps nailed all over the office, a touch he'd always admired. They passed the drive-in theater and laughed about experiences they'd had slipping in drive-ins when they were kids.

She had an apartment in a modest old house. It seemed the natural thing to kiss her a couple of times. She put her hand against his neck and smelled of a soft perfume.

"Look," he said, "I've got to write a speech. If I get through in time and you're not busy, why don't I give you a call tomorrow and we can celebrate my words to the farmers with a couple of beers and a little Indian wrestling and maybe a shoot-em-up movie?"

She let her tan hand slide down his arm and agreed, smiling.

He walked her to the house and waited until she latched the old fashioned screen door and then walked back down the concrete steps to the car. The house was on a comfortable street lined with live oaks. Through the tops of them he could see the sky stretched out wide and peaceful and rash with stars. Washington, when he thought of it, seemed like a long ago bad dream.

A tunnel of burned buildings like blackened hollowed eye sockets; walls leaning, metal gates gnarled, twisted, collapsed, contents mutilated, chewed and spit forth, strewn to mix with destruction and create abomination; there on the sidewalk, the streets no longer streets and sidewalks but trenches, alleys, pits, barricades, battlegrounds, a shattered kaleidoscope. Past great parks of rubble, steel girders reaching up, twisted into obscene gestures, great dying blackened monsters smoking torn cigars, Sunny moves. The gun weights her pocket.

The street lights long since gone, neon lights once illuminating bright wares now illuminate ruination. Occasional elongated strips of light along window shades indicate the possibility of life. Quiet, silence, only the sound of her steps, glass crunching beneath them, rubble kicked aside, stumbled over. It is curfew. The activity has passed elsewhere. But bodies remain, plastic, stripped, stiff, wigless, dismembered, numb as she. Torn objects, diseased streets, a boil burst, running sores laid bare.

Inside a building a dog whines. The sound nearly human, pleading painfully. Stumbling toward the sound, a burned name and DIS OUNT . . . the interior blackened. The door frame burned but intact except for the glass. Inside through the frame, catching her coat, a ripping sound, the smell of wet, burned wood. Another whine, a further step and the tear gas rises from the floor engulfing her, and she runs tripping on the door, falling, her hand catching her, pain, glass, bleeding, choking, her throat and nose burning, tears down her face, hiding in her arms, trying to clear the fumes. . . .

My friend and I could have helped you, she thinks, looking back toward the dog. I'm sorry.

A voice stern, loud, coming up the street through the rubble. Sunny presses herself against a still existent wall and waits straining through the smoke and her own tears to see the figure. The voice insistent, continuing, serious, conversing, the words meaningless. The woman is tall, stout, erect, carrying a purse, talking to no one beside her, holding no one's arm, her voice registering disapproval, gesturing toward the desolation around her. She stops periodically and calls out a name. She waits, her tall body turning slowly, surveying the alternate darkness and neon around her. Then she moves on talking.

Sunny watches her pass and disappear down the shadowy street, hears a shout, the sound of the soldiers down the block. . . .

In front of her a rat scurries from a decapitated mannequin and slithers across the street and into a burned building. Displaced. Burned out.

Poor rat. Even you don't deserve this.

She put her hand in her pocket and touched the cool gun and, comforted, she moved on, threading her way through the rubble.

Soon, soon, soon . . . not too much further, not too many blocks, her mind echoed. . . .

A helicopter drew near and again she waited against a building. The sound was deafening and brutal and somehow fitting. It hovered over the street like a monstrous horsefly, fanning the smoke, lights searching the ruins.

You could have caused this, you ugly, monstrous insect.

It swept on down the street and she walked on.

From a corner came the sounds of glass and voices. Three young boys paused as she passed, looking out at her curiously. The smell of liquor poured out onto the street, mingling with the smoke. Their bodies were decorated with store displays—a bare chest wrapped with corrugated cardboard, a cardboard crown set on a forehead. Behind them strips of neon illuminated the broken store. Glass covered the floor like sawdust, the shelves like mail-slots stood empty, the cash register lay spilled on the floor, its drawer hanging out.

Up the street music, dirgelike, discordant, issued from the darkness. There was a small light over a sign—The Brotherly Love Mission. There was no door, only an open doorway. Light from a back hallway barely illuminated the room strewn with metal chairs and one long table. Religious pictures hung on the wall untouched. In the rear of the room near the hallway a small old man with white wispy hair played the piano and sang.

> *Jesus, why are you lying there in the gutter*
> *Lipstick on your mouth, a pearl in your ear?* . . .
>
> *Why are you dragging your mother*
> *Up the twelve flights of stairs?* . . .

The old man stopped playing when he heard her footsteps behind him. Only his foot continued working the pedal up and down while he sat still, facing the piano, leaning forward slightly, studying music that wasn't there.

"Please," she said.

He turned and his worn old face seemed familiar to her.

"Please," she said, "you must know Timothy Rose. Where is he? Have you seen him?"

He turned, looking at her face as though searching for someone. There was a squeak in the pedal he worked up and down as though he were pumping breath into his body. He turned away in disappointment. His hands shook over the battered keys but he strained to hold them still until he struck a chord. The sound shook through the room and rang on, held by the pedal long after he had lifted his hands.

"Timothy Rose," she repeated, "where is Timothy Rose?"

His voice quivered when he spoke. "Timothy Rose sold guns and liquor and dope to the niggers. I told him, I said, Timothy Rose, the devil's got you by the gold cross. But he'd smile. God is with me, he'd say. You don't understand there's God in those things. That's all the God some people have, he'd say." The old man played a D flat on the piano.

"Where is he?" she asked.

He played the note again insistently. "Timothy Rose is dead," he said, ". . . Roland is gone. Timothy Rose died first. They carried Roland off this morning."

She leaned down looking into his face. "Timothy Rose is dead?" she whispered. His eyes glittered but seemed not to focus on her.

"Timothy Rose is dead, Roland is gone. . . ."

"How do you know Timothy Rose is dead?" She touched his shoulder. It was thin like a child's.

"Seen him," he said, looking at her now. He turned with the piano stool, it moaned beneath him. "They brung him in here." He raised a trembling finger and pointed toward the door. There was fear in his eyes as though he were reliving the scene. "Laid him on the table. . . ." He stared up at her, his eyes wild. "Had black on his hands, smeared all over 'em. But he had on that cross he wears. It was him all right. 'The cross, it weren't gold no more,' Roland said; 'see there. . . .' Roland's gone. . . ."

His voice broke and he let his head fall directly onto the piano so there was a clatter of notes. His shoulders shook.

"I'm sorry," she said.

"Roland's gone," he said. He raised his head and wiped his eyes with an old sock he pulled from his shirt pocket. "He was my best friend. They carried him off first thing this morning. I was taking care of him." He stared down at the piano keys as though the smooth ivory soothed him.

Sunny turned, feeling the gun fall against her leg.

"He's dead now and Timothy Rose is dead. John Kennedy is dead. My sister Marie is dead. She was a right pretty girl. . . ."

There were no windows in the building, only the door, so that it was close as a tomb. Sunny wiped the sweat from her forehead.

Timothy Rose is dead, she told herself.

The man seemed to have forgotten her and was playing chords again, but when she started walking away, he stopped.

"You see Roland, you tell him . . ." His voice died off and he began striking the chords again.

She started toward the door, winding her way through the overturned chairs and reading the signs on the walls. "Jesus will save you." "What have you done for your brother today?" "The Fountain of Blood Awaits You." "The End is Near."

She stopped beside the table where Timothy Rose had lain. It was gray metal and cool against her hand. She ran her fingers along the edge and touched them to her forehead.

"Oh, Timothy Rose," she wanted to cry out. "Timothy Rose, Timothy Rose, Timothy Rose."

When she reached the door the little man was singing again.

> *Jesus isn't what you think he is . . .*
> *He is me, he is you . . .*
> *He is little children on their way to school. . . .*

Outside in the street she glimpsed the moon full, bloated, and discolored through the smoky air. Below it a shorted gold neon flashed like a warning. She walked on nearing a residential section where the destruction grew less severe.

Nearly there, she told herself, nearly there, nearly there.

She walked thinking of all the strange streets she would never see, all the crazy, sick jumbled streets full of beautiful, mournful, happy people she'd never hear laugh or cry or shout, never touch or talk to or even exchange glances with. She wished she had spent her whole life stopping people and talking to them and asking them how they were. She wished she'd spent all those years in school talking to people and finding out about them. She thought how all those streets and people and rooms and doors she'd never see and those she'd walked by without ever noticing, ended in the same place, nowhere; just where she was, nowhere; and it didn't matter who was waiting for you somewhere or what alley you hid in or what shortcut you took or what disguise you assumed or who your daddy was, or what name you called yourself, or what kind of hat you wore, or what kind of guaranteed-by-Good Housekeeping antiseptic you sprinkled on your body, or what you carried in your pocket, they'd all end in the same dark doorway. The only choice in the world you had was smiling now and then along the way and sometimes getting there sooner.

An old-fashioned red-striped column stood in front of the building on the corner of Thirteenth Street. Large trailing plants sat wilted in the windows of the barber shop, glass sprinkled about their leaves; glass littered the linoleum floor and the leather barber chairs sat empty and burned. Next door a carry-out had been looted and partially burned, but the floors above them seemed unscathed.

Sunny searched the fronts of the stores looking for the addresses, but they were gone, broken away with the glass or burned away, and then in the darkness she saw the door between the two buildings. She moved closer and saw in the entryway the glass case.

"MOTHER MYRA, SPIRITUAL HEALER AND AD-VISOR." In one corner was a cross, in the other a star. "You who pass do not turn away. I can help you. Upstairs. Third floor." One of the handbills was tacked below it and then a cardboard hand pointed toward the door.

Sunny pushed the metal handle. The door was heavy and fitted unevenly on its hinges. It fell back, scraping on the floor inside. There was a red light at the end of the hall where a door behind the stairs faced her. She closed the door behind her. The place smelled of smoke and bad cooking, and she leaned back, feeling her stomach rise. Afraid she was going to be sick there inside the door, she swallowed, breathing deeply. Her hand throbbed and she rubbed it against the door so the pain brought tears to her eyes and the nausea passed.

Mother Myra, I have come . . .

The narrow wooden stairs groaned and creaked beneath her. She leaned on the bannister and felt it sway and she drew back moving slowly, trying to make no sound, afraid of being stopped or found out, but only a spindly cat scrambled past her.

On the second landing she stopped, out of breath and lightheaded, and wiped her forehead on the sleeve of her coat. There was blood there somewhere on the sleeve from the cut on her hand. There seemed to be no air in the building. She heard a creak and a door opened a crack to watch her and she put her hand in her pocket to feel the gun there.

I was so afraid . . . have you ever been afraid . . . really afraid . . .

On the third floor there was another red overhead light illuminating the two doors. On one a printed card was tacked to the door. "Mother Myra. Please knock."

The surface of the door was scarred and wrinkled beneath her knuckles. There was no sound but the faint voice of a radio somewhere below. She knocked again louder.

Please, please, please . . .

When the voice came, it seemed to come from far away through many halls and corridors, muffled and winding, a strange, raspy voice captured in the prison of stale rooms and drained of life or sex.

"Please, I'd like to talk to you," Sunny whispered, leaning against the door.

There was a movement on the other side, a rustling, and a chain dropped and the door opened a crack. It was dark inside.

"Lock the door behind you," the voice said moving away.

Sunny opened the door slowly and passed into an entry the end of which was covered with dark curtains. There was a musty smell about the room and she had the feeling she was walking through cobwebs. She pulled the door to behind her and slid the lock.

My name is Sunny Tidwell. . . .

She waited in the darkness until an orange light appeared around the curtains and a chair scraped and the voice called her to come inside. Her hand brushed the cold wall as she pulled the curtain back. Then she glanced at the woman sitting in the middle of the room at a table, but her glance veered away instinctively and through her mind passed the memory of a woman's face, long ago, a paisley of scars.

The room itself was of small relief. In the corner was an altar with candles and a picture of the Blessed Virgin and above it around a crucifix hung the pictures of other saints. The room was small and filled with dark shabby furniture laden with scarves and littered with combs and bottles and ointments and powders and dried and dead flowers in cheap glass vases and the stuffed head of a black cat mounted on a wooden plaque. Pinned to the curled, discolored wallpaper were photographs, newspaper clippings, and magazine pictures of all manner of mayhem; scenes of riots and killings and accidents and dwarfs and deformed children and dead animals straight-pinned to the wall like the butterfly wings of a lepidopterist. On the bureau was a snapshot of a child, younger but familiar, and somewhere in the maze of the wall was a mirror where she glimpsed herself reflected in the dim orange light, and hardly recognizing the face, she thought for a second of the image as one more of the atrocities pinned to the wall. Seeking some relief she turned away toward the two windows covered with sheer yellowed curtains and unmatching drapes. But the woman who'd been waiting as though expecting the survey made a slight nod of her head toward the chair opposite her, and Sunny, sensing Mother Myra's direction, sat down, catching her foot a moment on the cord of the orange lava light sitting in the middle of the table. The light alone illuminated the room, spreading a circle of orange glow around them. Its bright, shiny gold base was incongruous with the dilapidation around it, but its ugliness, the slow, constant oozing motion of the orange matter, fitted into the stillness as if it were a last breath in a room of the dead.

Sunny raised her eyes, forcing herself to look at the woman, telling herself at first it was a mask, but knowing it was not, simply thinking that momentarily to protect herself. She had seen a similar face somewhere, not so grotesque, but the face of an outcast. Now prepared, she studied the woman's features. They were heavy, uneven, almost as though they were greatly swollen. Her face was sandy and mottled, her cheeks variegated as though the skin had peeled away over and over again. Her eyes and eyelashes were colorless, like straw, and her hair was like a ball of eggshell wool pressed on her head as a helmet. The face seemed to be a rubber ball, lifeless except for the broad red painted lips and the pale eyes that had her under surveillance.

The woman moved, feeling in the pocket of her skirt and drawing out a loose cigarette. She put it in the side of her mouth, reached for a match, lighted it, waved the match, and with a careless flick of her wrist dropped it onto the table. Her lids drooped heavily as though with great fatigue and sweat stood on her forehead.

"You come from the dark?" the woman asked her. Her voice was tired.

Sunny shook her head, not understanding.

"You come from the street?"

"Yes. . . ."

"It goes bad," she said. "In my dreams God cries for us. I hear sobbing. I tremble for all people. This world will end soon. 'Babylon the great is fallen . . . and is become the habitation of the devils and the hold of every foul spirit and a cage of every unclean and hateful bird.' . . ." She turned her head slightly and there was a queer, quick oscillation of her eyes.

Sunny looked down as the malformations of clouds rose slowly in the liquid of the lava light and separated again, and broke and descended slowly, oozing their way through the fluid mysteriously like some microscopic miracle.

Timothy Rose is dead . . . is dead. . . . Bless me, mother, for I have sinned.

"Why do you come to me?" the woman asked. Her heavy breasts rose and fell beneath a tangle of many colored glass beads. "God clad you in white," she said as though it were an accusation. "But if you come to me for help I can help you. Lots of white people walked in that door with the devil sitting on their shoulder and I helped God to take it off. . . . What kind of trouble you got?"

"Bad," Sunny said quietly, "bad, bad trouble."

"All trouble's bad," the woman said, "and everybody thinks his is worse. You been living in the dark world, I can see that . . . you coming here now. That can be bad trouble. . . ."

She turned and looked about the room and again her eyes made a strange erratic movement.

"I know it well, being bound to darkness with eyes that can't live in the day. No power can change what God marked in the womb. No power or charm or potion or prayer. But when he blew the black from my skin in the womb and put me into the darkness, he give me powers. And I have the power to see the darkness and the light and the struggle. And I know the night. You understand what I mean?"

Sunny nodded.

"I know the night. I know the women walking the streets and the men staggering and the young men running and later in the early hours the old people and the hungry dogs searching the cans. . . . But in the night eyes are not mirrors. There are many monsters in the night . . . many monsters. So I learned to live with it well. . . ."

She stared at the scarred table, her eyes fixed until Sunny thought she had forgotten her or gone into a trance, but suddenly she raised her eyes and looked at her interestedly.

"The Bible says, 'Let him remember the days of darkness;

for they shall be many.' . . ." Her voice was low and she stared again into space as if seeing all the dark days passing. . . .

"What else is there?" Sunny asked. "All I know is darkness and dying and that nothing resolves itself. It just ends." She glanced at the woman's eyes and then away, wondering what they were saying and why she was there.

"So you've seen bad trouble," the woman said. "There's some people only learn of the darkness in brief dreams. They don't understand about nights that never end. A soul can be saved or spent in learning that."

The cigarette burned to her fingers and the woman dropped it into a glass cup on the floor.

"And what do you say to someone with the worst trouble . . . ?" Sunny asked. "Someone who's killed someone?" She said it easily, not even pausing on the word.

The woman's voice was stronger when she spoke.

"A man who takes the life of another spends his own soul." Her head nodded slowly and she looked at Sunny from under heavy lids. "And the Lord said to Cain, 'The voice of thy brother's blood crieth unto me from the ground. And now thou art cursed from the earth . . . a fugitive and a vagabond shalt thou be. . . .' And the Lord said, 'Whosoever slayeth Cain vengeance shall be taken on him sevenfold.' . . ."

Sunny turned away and saw her face reflected there in the dim orange light . . . still and cold like wax.

"Yes, I see," she said, "I see. . . ." She closed her eyes, feeling only the presence of the woman and the room around her as though she had disappeared.

"When you came in," Mother Myra said, "you looked at me and were afraid. But you looked at yourself and were afraid and I knew you see yourself in darkness and you had trouble. Many come here who have a trouble. I can help them with candles and tell them which saint to pray to and give them johnny root or dragon's blood and lodestones. But you are not one of them. There is no candle, no root to work that kind of darkness. There is no relief except to become a saint or to seek that which dulls the senses, a potion of the gods for those who are not made of saintly cloth. That is all I can offer you."

She lifted her straw eyebrows and watched Sunny stare into the orange light. A bulbous cloud broke slowly and disappeared.

"I raised a boy," Mother Myra said. "He learned ugliness and hate and he couldn't live with it. I watched his rage grow, the devil blowing on the coals. Each inch he grew, his rage grew a pound in his heart. He was punished and with each punishment his hate grew till the devil had him snared and his soul was black as his skin. . . . Do you believe the dead come back?" she asked Sunny.

"I don't know."

"They do," she said. "You have to wait for them in the dark. I hear him whisper in this very room. He comes and whispers but that is all that's left, him whispering in the dark and a boy that wanders the streets looking for his daddy he only remembers in a box. . . ."

Her chair scraped against the floor and Mother Myra put her hands on the table and leaned toward Sunny, and Sunny saw for the first time the emerald ring Norris had shown her. It glistened newly on her little finger, its diamonds encircling it, sparkling bright and with a purity in the haunted room.

She thought of his ankles thin, like a bird's, small and gentle.

"Norris . . ." she said. She met the woman's strange light eyes that seemed to rest apart on her face with no connection, and the eyes again made a frantic movement in the colorless surroundings and Sunny felt the woman had divined what she was about to say.

"He's dead."

For the first time since she'd entered the room she felt the gun heavy in her lap as she watched the emerald move to the woman's face where her thick hand clasped her mouth. Other rings climbing her short fingers shone dully in the orange light; her fingers pressed, distorting her face. Her eyes clung to Sunny's, growing wide and red like fires while her body rocked back and forth.

Sunny's knees trembled when she stood.

"I'm sorry. . . . I'm sorry," she whispered again.

She backed from the table looking around her at the room and the woman rocking there, at the accumulation of those trophies of suffering brought there day by day, pinned to the walls, each of them contributing its own force. And then she had come, she who should be impaled there alongside them, the largest filament. Suddenly she felt the power, the evil she had carried with her into the room and she knew that only madmen and the truly evil had known that power.

She turned and pushed through the dark curtains and opened the lock and fled into the mad darkness where she might hide.

 VIII

The trunk of the Mustang was stuffed with cases of liquor and bottles of wine stacked loose around the sides. Dollar a bottle, they said. I want a bottle of scotch, I told them. There were two of them all dressed up and pretty high themselves. You ain't gonna drink that all alone, are ya, baby, they asked me. I don't drink any other way nowadays, I told them.

"I put my hands in my pockets half hoping they'd get really fresh so I could bring out my black companion and show them I was more than meets the eye, but they were more interested in the money they were getting for the hot liquor, so I left with a bottle and four dollars. Four dollars and change in the world, and I gave four dollars to the man downstairs for the room. Pay in advance was the rule. So it came out about even, which is nice. I like things to come out even, like eating roast beef and mashed potatoes and corn. I was always careful so there'd be some for each bite. Like eating Mexican food or pizza and coming out with more food than beer; it ruins the whole entire meal.

"So here I am on the fifth and top floor of the Marvel Hotel. So far I've not seen any marvels. You see, I never learn. Why should the Marvel Hotel have anything to do with marvels! It's just a word, maybe a goal, maybe not, just a label like everything else. Marvel. What is a marvel? You say the word over and over and it grows strange and you think maybe you're mispronouncing it. Marvel, what a strange word.

"So here I am in the Marvel Hotel, room 5-E and I'm composing this message and I'm going to stick it in the scotch bottle when I'm finished with it, and sail these words out the window on the waves of smoke that cover this city. Some day when all the smoke is gone this will float up to some gutter and some unhappy man will bend over and pick it up and read it. He'll go home to his wife and say, I found the damnedest thing today in the gutter, and she'll say, you must be the only man in Washington who picks up bottles in the gutters, you fool. Someday they'll cart you to the loony bin. So he will tell her no more and only he will know. But he'll die one day, a heart attack on the street in front of a cleaner's, and no one will try mouth-to-mouth resuscitation because he's old and repulsive and has bad teeth. Then no one will know about this note, unless maybe some day he gets drunk before he dies and tells some bartender or some drunken neighbor about this damn thing he found in a bottle in the gutter."

I put my hand down, resting, and look at the dull green walls of the room. It is difficult writing. It is hard to control, just like everything. What I want to say gets mixed up, mixed up with what comes out on the paper. Classy joint this Marvel Hotel, this brown-stained paper. Must be the only person in the world ever wrote anything in room 5-E of the Marvel Hotel.

Maybe I should write individual notes. Dear Daddy, here I am in the Marvel Hotel looking for marvels to occur. Legislate one for me quickly. I was such a pain-in-the-ass to you. You said so yourself. I'm sorry about that. I wish I could have been that sunny child. I really do. Not that I wish I'd have been just what you wanted me to be, that would be a lie, and I'm truthful as hell today, but I wish I could have been a little happier. Why couldn't I be a peacemaker? I mean Joan of Arc did lots of big things. If I could ask you one thing I'd say, do you really believe all those things you say? I don't mean those things to me and mother about respect and scheming behind your back to ruin your career, but those things you say to people in speeches. Do you picture God as a white American? Did you ever think about how you loved states' rights, democracy, the Liberty Lobby, our men in the armed forces fighting for freedom, freedom-loving countries, and yet you warred against your own family. Think about that, Daddy dear. That is obscene.

Of course if I asked you that to your face you'd be mad, wouldn't you, and it would be just another wrangle. Maybe I could disguise myself as FDR or John Foster Dulles or someone else you respected and see what you'd say. Can we really believe that differently, you and me, flesh and blood tied, sitting at the same supper table all those horrible screaming years?

Well, Daddy, I'll not end my last communication with you on that same old note. Now I'll tell you something you really want to hear. Pretty soon you'll not have to worry about me, old dear. I'll be out of your constituency forever and ever and maybe I'll come back to haunt you. Would you listen to me if I were a ghost and came back and sat on your desk blowing your papers about? How funny that would be! If your papers start blowing, just look around for me, Daddy. I'll be the only ghost in the room who has eyebrows just like yours.

But I'm just going on, going on, making no sense at all, no sense a'tall, as they say in the homeland. I've got to get back to the business at hand, as my father would say. The Marvel Hotel. Here I am marvelous in the Marvel Hotel.

"You see there are only five rooms on each floor and then only bedrooms on the top three floors. On the second (and I'm talking about the Marvel Hotel) is the National Wig Company and a recording studio that may be closed down. It looks very closed. There is a chain on the door and it has a dusty unused quality about it. Of course there is a generally dusty, unused quality about this hotel, but about the Crown Recording Company in particular. On the third floor is the photographic studio that has brown photos in the glass case outside. For two-fifty, a sign says, you can get passport photos while you wait. But it does not look as though its clients are the type who'd need passport photos, except maybe as cheap Christmas presents, if you know what I mean. In the window is a girl in an evening gown smiling too widely since her gums show above her teeth. She wears a strapless gown and her arms are too fat and there is a roll of flesh where the stays are pinching between her arm and the top of the gown, but no cleavage. Her hair is teased high and lacquered with hair spray. She has rhinestone earrings (drops) and a look of hope. She is probably not a virgin. She is one of those innocent and unattractive girls who giggles about sex and pretends to be afraid and is won easily and sweatily. She looks at you smiling, waiting for some young man to come say he loves her. She does not particularly care if they live happily ever after. She will trudge through life in her girdle not expecting too much, not getting too much, and she'll be fat, trying to diet all her life, until she dies when she will reduce with no effort at all.

"Also on the third floor is the office of a lawyer named O. Mallory Cunningham. O. Mallory Cunningham. Dear O. Mallory Cunningham. Your name is a delight to a strong and vigorous mouth. It is very tiring for a southern mouth, pursing one's lips and then retreating rapidly so the mouth must move like a Frenchman's. O? Oliver? Olivia? Yes. Probably a woman would call herself O. Mallory. Very nice. How do you do, O. Mallory Cunningham? Mrs. Cunningham, will you help me? Olivia? Would you like my seat here on this bus? You must be tired dispensing justice all day the way you do. O Mallory, you are a pain-in-the-ass!

"Directly beside the door of O. Mallory Cunningham's office is the Federal Secretarial Service. 'We do Résumés and Forms.' Perhaps that means that O. Mallory is Oliver Mallory and the Federal Secretary is Olivia Jennyanydots and sometimes on rainy afternoons, with the honking of cars, roars of buses below, and the droning of planes above, they lie on the torn plastic sofa and make love, their bare bodies sticking against the torn plastic. But maybe they are too tired to worry with bare bodies and they simply lie there amid rumpled clothing trying to attain some bit of tired ecstasy that drowns out all cars, buses, planes, rattles of the old creaking elevator and cries from the fifth floor. Good luck to you both. And all you sad people along the elevator route of the Marvel Hotel.

"I will tell you my name because it doesn't matter. My name is Sunny Tidwell. What is a name? A hell of a lot, let me tell you. Plain as any name can be—Sunny. It is a name that grows old and particularly tiring on one's own lips. Who can grow old as Sunny! It is impossible. Sunny, to say it is a pain and a strain."

Downstairs, cleverly, I put Eleanor Worthington. So here I am, Daddy, little Eleanor. Demure, sweet, in my dotted swiss dress, twirling my parasol up here on the platform while the band plays . . . a sweet Eleanor, a loyal Kappa Kappa Gamma-ray, she is. All the little Eleanors she knows will be one, too. I'm so sweet, I smell good, little Eleanor.

Of course, he didn't believe it, not the manager, a gray, unshaven man in dirty brown pants with hairs protruding from his ears and nose who only looked at me a moment and turned back to the television set. He did not mention that I had no bag, though I did swing my arms nonchalantly to show him I had none, expecting him to say something. I'm just passing through, I told him. I'd always wanted to say that. Just passing through like food; I'll go out the bottom, man, only I didn't say that. I was Eleanor and she just wouldn't. I wished immediately I'd signed something like Zelda or Mattie or Françoise. It would have been nice having people look at you as a Zelda. But I didn't think of that in time; that is the tragedy of my life. I always think of the right words afterwards. Isn't that right, Fletcher? No, as a matter of fact. I don't think of the right words, even afterwards.

The redcap-and-elevator operator noticed I didn't have bags. Twice on the way up in the bumpy elevator he opened his mouth to say something but didn't. Perhaps he simply had adenoids and breathed like a fish. I think not. He wasn't sure about me. He was very young and had sallow skin. If he had lived in Texas, his mother would have raised hollyhocks in the front yard.

There was something fresh about the way he looked at me. He had white pimples in his chin and very blond hair. You could tell he was a big sports fan. Why, he knew baseball statistics and would fight over them. He was eating a Twinkie and the wrapping and the crumbs rested on the stool inside the elevator. He stood up, letting the wrapping sit there. There was cream stuffing on the corner of his mouth and he wiped it off with the back of his hand. Women never do that, wipe their mouths with the back of their hands. We do it more delicately—with the thumb and the index finger, no smearing the lipstick that way.

When he pulled the old metal gate and opened the door on the fifth floor and I passed by him, he smelled of hair oil. Who in the world smells of hair oil nowadays, I wanted to say to him. He stuffed the rest of the Twinkie in his mouth, then he stopped the elevator and opened the gate so that we had to step up a good six inches to get out. He led the way down the peeling gray corridor, chewing the Twinkie, and opened the door to 5-E and raised his hand in half apology, half goodbye, still chewing.

"In this room I feel safe. It is small and there is nothing to hide. There is a shallow closet, but with the door straight open, I can see its walls. There is no rug except a small one that was by the bed and now it hangs across the back of the small wooden chair so that there is nothing concealed on the floor. Outside the window it is gray, smoky gray. Everywhere I look it is through a dirty window. On top of the dresser is a Gideon Bible, a remnant of some conviction become ritual. The bathroom is down the hall and belongs to others, too. It is better that way. A bathroom alone is a responsibility. When I went there a roach was occupying it. It scurried out from the corner and sat in the middle of the floor, wiggled its antennae measuring my strength and then slid slowly under the radiator finding me no powerful antagonist.

"After that, Mr. Oppenheimer (that is what I'll call you, if you don't mind, though I know it's a trillion to one chance that it is really your name), I decided to call Ronald Kildale. It was only fair that I deliver my testimony, I thought. I planned to tell him what I thought of him: Ronald Kildale, you son-of-a-bitch. You are mean to people on your program. They don't care what you think. Don't you know they just want to say something, to be heard somewhere? You fool. Do you think your replies have any effect? You try to make sense of people's loneliness and fear and get mad and make fun of them. You are a cruel, mean, awful man, Ronald Kildale.

"And then I was going to speak to all those callers, those people listening at home by their radios, all those women ironing, and all those men on their stoops who don't have jobs. I was going to say to them: Beware of the Ronald Kildales who try to enforce their logic on you. Just because Ronald Kildale has some kind of position, a power so that with a flick of the switch he can end your thoughts, cease your communication, don't think that really means that he's anything better than you are. I know all about those people in the newspaper, those people in government clubs and cloakroom cliques. They don't know any more than we do—you and me, people who look out their windows and buy their own groceries and use No-Roach. Don't believe what they say unless you examine it first, each word separately. Chances are two to one it's a lie. . . . I was going to really tell them the truth, I was going to really knock Ronald Kildale for a loop but they wouldn't let me talk.

"I'm sorry, but we have six callers waiting and it's unlikely that Mr. Kildale will be able to speak to more than three of them as it is. The program is nearly over, the woman said. She had very good diction. What part of the country are you from, I asked her, always impressed with good diction.

"She was impolite, too. I had to call back with my last dime. Listen, I said, it's important that I talk. It is a matter of life or death. I've got to say something. But she wasn't interested in life or death. She probably didn't believe in it. I've been listening to Ronald Kildale for months and months, I said, and this is the first time I've called and I have a right to talk. It's my turn, I told her. Turn about fair play. I asked her if she could repeat the Bill of Rights, and she hung up again. It seems to me that everything has been quiet since then. Since then I have rested, all but my mind.

"I'll write this down. It does seem that things around me are whole, integrated, sensible. Did someone tell me a daisy has twenty-three petals, always? Does each petal know this?

Or does it rest there, spending its life not knowing it is part of a perfect twenty-three? But then what would a daisy know? The chenille bedspread is even, made so by machine, made by man. I press my face to it and come up with neat rows except that my face being irregular does not make for neat rows. That is the whole problem, I suppose.

"This room is small. If my body breaks open, all the fluids will spill easily across the sloping linoleum and pool around the closet door. That way it might be possible to save them, to lie in the stream. My body is a sponge and could soak them up.

"I lie on the bed atop the chenille spread, rose-pink like thousands and thousands of housecoats distributed all over the country, giving me a kinship with all those ladies, the tie pulled across their waists giving their backs a nice compact look. Think of all the women who've eaten scrambled eggs in their pink chenille bathrobes, who've gotten the sleeves wet washing dishes afterward. The feel of that chenille flapping around their ankles over their nylon gowns, over their beginning-to-sag breasts, their beginning-to-varicose veins, running children off to school, sitting down and smoothing their uncombed hair, and feeling the damp sleeves against their pale arms, picking up cups of coffee with unmanicured hands and going upstairs later and trying to change, dropping the chenille on the floor, then hanging it on a hook where it looks like a big faded rag, but never really getting away, out from under that chenille bathrobe. Whole generations of women have been demoralized by chenille bathrobes. I looked for one once, wanting to slop around till noon in an old faded rose chenille robe and watch soap operas, but I couldn't find one. It was too premeditated, anyway. One shouldn't dress for one's role. Besides, chenille robes are part of the past that is over. Now they are nylon dusters and running your hand over them is like touching cellophane-covered fruit. You can't get through. If I had one slogan for the women of the world, I would tell them to throw away their nylon dusters. At least under chenille you could feel yourself there—a little bumpy perhaps, but there. Under nylon you can't be sure.

"I am sitting now in this room and writing very carefully. My handwriting has always been rather poor and I am making a sincere effort to be careful. When I was in the first grade, our teacher Mrs. Hunnicut had lost her only son the year before. He was drunk in his old gray Plymouth and passed out on the tracks and a train hit him. She revenged herself by teaching us the wrong way to write so that our whole class wrote without the index finger over the pencil. She'd never taught like that before. When the parents discovered the disaster it was too late.

"But if you, Mr. Oppenheimer, cannot read this, that is all right, too. I suppose that it will not matter so much. This pencil is a number two Blue Mirror. It is yellow with a short dirty eraser. Let me assure you this is an all-American pencil driven by an all-American who grew up singing 'God Bless America.' Did you know, Mr. Oppenheimer, that during World War II only Kate Smith was allowed to use the President's entrance to Union Station—besides the President, of course. That's the kind of useful information one learns in Washington, D.C. I do not remember that war, but I remember Kate Smith singing. We had a record and I'd turn it on and I'd jump on the easy chair, a foot on each arm and sing at the top of my voice along with Kate, over and over, even after Kate had stopped until Mother would run me out the door. How patriotic I felt! It made me want to grow up and kill somebody.

"I loved that song until my father made me hate it. He made me sing only moving my mouth with the record going in the background. I got all dressed up, thinking I was really going to sing for his friends, then he sprang it on me at the last minute. I didn't know I'd mind so much but they laughed. I hadn't realized it was all a joke.

"This room is green. I would guess that seventy percent of cheap rooms are green. The floor is brown-painted linoleum. The furniture is that bulbous 1940 modern and there are seventeen cigarette burns including three on the night table, four on the bureau and ten on the dresser. (I am big on statistics.) I have never understood why they'd put both a dresser and a bureau in such a hotel. Does anyone truly live here? Think of all the bureaus in the country never filled, living all their existence with empty drawers. The dresser has a cracked mirror. The crack runs diagonally like a flash of lightning. I have not used the ceiling light so I don't know if it works. But it has a plastic shade with gold streaks in it. It's the kind that clamps over a naked light bulb. You can buy one in any dime store. In fact, anything you can buy in one dime store can be bought in all other dime stores. It is absolutely communistic. Should be investigated.

"I have heard that they must be very careful about protrusions from the ceilings and walls in places like this because so many people come to hang themselves in hotels. Of course, rooms like this lend themselves to such thoughts, all those empty drawers, and probably a good twenty-five percent of the people never thought of it till they got inside the room. (You see I am very good on statistics. They can be fun, if you don't take them too seriously, don't you think, Mr. Oppenheimer?)

"The thing that is really wonderful about this room is the picture of the Indian. You know that picture of the Indian on the horse with his arms raised and he has a wonderful trail of feathers down his back. That was on the wall of my grandmother's home. I would look at that Indian for hours, but I never remember asking about him. Why didn't I ask? There are so many things I should have asked. Why was I content to look? How could I have wondered so peacefully? Why did I have to wait until years later to begin asking? Perhaps I will address this Indian directly. 'Who are you, Indian?' I'll ask him."

I rest my hand on the Marvel Hotel paper. Outside it is growing into twilight. I lean over the bed and lift my friend the scotch up beside me and take a long drink. It will have to be finished before the letter goes inside. Lots of responsibilities I have here. I hold the bottle before the bedside light. Two inches left.

The cut throbs. I douse it with scotch and grit my teeth as it burns. Grit your teeth, it won't hurt, my mother says. Grit your teeth. Did you grit your teeth, Mother? I must remember to grit my teeth. My hand hurts a lot but I don't think of it all the time. Preoccupied is what I am. I say it out loud and my voice is hollow in the empty room. My stomach growls unhappily. In the broken mirror I can see myself. Surprised I am at how I look. So thin. Hair greasy, unkempt, neck and arms unfamiliar, a part of another person, a stranger. My neck and arms had always been like my mother's. It was startling, the duplication. Eerie as though there was someone else living here, too, but in the mirror they are strange, plastic, like those dismembered mannequins on the street, like the stems of very artificial flowers.

I examine the cut on my hand and think of a gunshot wound. When I was a child I dreamed once I was shot. Psychic I am. I remember the wound, the pull of the skin around the wound like an anal opening, ugly and raw.

I didn't see Norris's wounds. Is that what I dreamed? Did I dream mine or his or will they be the same?

"You see, Mr. Oppenheimer, this blood from the cut on my hand is not just mine. I don't think I'll ever quit bleeding. I don't understand what happened. Have you ever been afraid, really afraid, Mr. Oppenheimer? Afraid can be a sin . . .

you can be so afraid. . . . Did it really matter so much to me? No. So why?

"What equals death, Mr. Oppenheimer? Guilt? Suffering? Cutting my arms and bleeding on and on, bleeding all the blood till there's no more and it pools there in front of the closet door? Not quite. It's got to be a declaration, you see. It's got to be lying out there on the street for someone to think about. I had been going to tell Ronald Kildale, but he wouldn't let me talk. At least you'll know, Mr. Oppenheimer, you'll understand that there's more than that girl with the black gun in her hand and the hole in her chest. Unlabeled she may be, except to herself. Shall I pin a note to my shirt? No, you will know, you and all these ghosts in this room who hung from the closet pole and Mother Myra maybe."

There are lights on the street now. Barefooted, feet cool against the linoleum, I go to the window carrying the bottle. Ah, a view of the city through the smoky haze of destruction! A Monet nightmare. Poor deserted streets. Only cops. Many buildings here still standing, saved for the slow death of rotting and decay. On the roof next door yellow water in a tank bubbles. Across the street is a movie theater, closed, the door to the ticket booth ajar. A cheap girlie theater with glossy black and white photos on the outside with strips of tape to save the world's modesty. What a nice place, that ticket booth! Selling tickets to the sad, sick, lonely, unloved. A man moves inside the glass doors and then the marquee comes on, bright and beckoning as if it had something promising to show.

I feel the grit beneath my elbows, the cracked paint of the ledge. I drink from the bottle and see a man in a building across the alley watching, but when I look toward him he turns away quickly.

The least you could do is smile and wave. That would have been the nice thing to do. After all, you can never tell who I might be. Why, look who I am! He moves away and all that is left in the window are two green file cabinets in the background. . . .

"Hello again, Mr. Oppenheimer. Here I am back with you. It is strange how much longer some moments are than others. These moments aware of the mass of my body, its weight against the bed, the feel of skin and bones moving against the paper, the monotony of my breathing, these are long, slow moments. Time should be relative to its density. These long moments in this room are not equal to others. The shortest moments are when you are in love, I mean really hung-up on somebody."

I remember when time went very fast with Fletcher. Oh, Fletchering, how nice. But it never lasts, does it? It changes and there's that self-consciousness and that kind of guilt and accusations and it's all a weight and a chore and a lie despite those nice warm, sleepy moments. Your body was so warm and nice, Fletcher.

The elevator creaks and the gate is pulled back and left to slam. Footsteps toward the door. A knock.

The white erupted face stares past the chain. He leans forward so that his breath like sour milk meets me. He stares at me a minute, his dull eyes weighing the possibilities.

"The manager says to tell you the curfew goes on in about an hour and if you're going to get out and eat you'd better go." He stood awaiting some response.

"Okay. Thanks." I start to push the door to. His foot stops it.

"Say, there's a good bar right across the street next to the theater, has a good bacon and tomato if you're looking for somewheres. Estelle runs the bar," he said. "Tell her Stevie sent ya over. Maybe I'll join ya." He cocked his thin head.

I close the door and wait for him to move away, feeling his disappointment through the door.

Well, you see the way it is, Stevie, I'd bleed all over you and I'm not so good at such things anyway, you know, I have to be all involved, and really I'm a snob about men. Besides, I have the feeling you're just playing. I bet evenings you tell girl friends in cheap bars how you laid all the hotel guests that day.

Maybe that is unkind. Unkind, indeed, I am, Stevie. You don't know the half of it. Another long swallow of scotch, please.

"Mr. Oppenheimer, I would like to ask you to be extremely kind. Let's make a pact. Had we ever known one another, it might have been a perfect relationship. We would have loved one another desperately, romantically. We might have stayed lovely and handsome and always laughed at one another and ended arguments with great sex scenes, just like the movies. Please whenever you feel depressed think of how we might have made it together. Don't you think that might help?"

Personally, I've loved lots of people. Girls at slumber parties I told secrets to, and men, and men, lovely men on planes carrying briefcases, and walking down Connecticut Avenue with their hats on, and boys in their tight levis swinging their cars around in small Texas towns. All those wonderful boys who'll grow into men with families and fat bellies and hemorrhoids. If only I had postcards I'd write some of them. Dear Joe, I loved you that summer when we went fishing on the Red River and sat on that cliff in the sun. I loved you and you never knew. But I want you to know now.

I drink the last swallow of scotch. It has a strange finality about it and I want to hug the bottle to me, it being the only thing that seems alive, but then I think of the gun. I will hug that to me and it will be alive and warm and responsive; the last fuck I'll ever have, that gun. I prop the bottle on the pillow next to me.

"All I ask, Mr. Oppenheimer, is that you don't laugh at what I've written. I know that probably some kid will pick it up and read it and laugh, or just pick it up and break the bottle and not even read it. But that's the chance we take, isn't it? Or then maybe no one will pick it up at all ever and there won't be anything left.

"So good luck to you, Mr. Oppenheimer. Could you believe I love you simply from having talked to you for so long?"

I roll the pages scroll-like until they will slide inside the bottle. Once inside, they expand and it looks very attractive. Maybe Mr. Oppenheimer will set it on his bar and it will become a conversation piece, but he'll say, no, there's writing on it but I never read it. Somehow I was afraid.

Such an attractive bottle is bound to be appreciated.

I lie back and close my eyes and wish for something warm there on the bed beside me. Timothy Rose, you touched me last. Where are you? Are you just gone, you who prepared yourself? You must have known you were going to die, getting yourself all saved and full of faith and hope at the end. Did you hear the angels' wings? Are you a spirit? Surely you'd come see me. Why don't you show yourself? Make me feel warm. Here it is, hot in this room and I feel my body warm and perspiring but inside I'm so coldly apart I'm in Alaska. You were such a silly man, Timothy Rose. Should I have taken you more seriously? Tried to understand you better? Is there anybody anywhere to take seriously? But you would understand me now. You know about these things I never understood—blood for blood and all that. Penance. Why, that's one of those words I thought I knew, but didn't.

Inspection time. Under the bed there are shoes. Three buttons on the shirt. One, two, three, one gone. The hand aches, aches, aches. Rewrap the towel around it. There must be glass inside it. The bottle inside the pocket, its green head protruding only slightly. The gun on the other side, lovely black body fitting nicely in my hand, the shells into the cartridge nicely, thank you. See, it will work again. Ready, aim. . . .

Now to go. Goodbye, green room. Close the door. Down the hall. Push the button. Wait. Push again. Through the dirty glass doors the cables slide. Finally the door opens, the white face of the boy.

I'm stepping on after all. Only I don't want to be a bottle riding along.

"Do you like being a bottle?" I ask him.

He is chewing gum and smoking a cigarette at once. Seeks oral satisfaction, this kid. He looks at me like I'm crazy.

"Bottle," he says with a glottal stop. "I ain't no bottle."

I press the bottle against me and feel the gun against my leg.

"You only got fifteen minutes," he says going down.

"That's plenty of time," I tell him.

He stops, taking his time landing but still stopping inches below the floor. He pulls the gate back and turns toward me not opening the door yet.

"You gonna get shot, you not back in fifteen minutes." He smirks and pulls the doors back.

"Oh, they don't shoot movie stars," I say to him as I pass.

The elevator slams behind me and the kid begins whistling a tune.

I leave the key on the counter. The manager doesn't look up. He is watching a Baltimore channel which is fuzzy and it requires all his concentration. I walk across the worn red rug patched with black tape and think of the empty ticket booth across the street. It would be nice there, protected but looking out on the street. A real museum piece I'd be. See! See! It would be like shouting. I could leave the bottle in the gutter and then cross the street and go inside and sit on that stool for all the world to see and hug that black companion to my heart. I bet I'll meet up with the scream that's been waiting all these nights. I'll show them there are open-mouthed mummies everywhere.

Marvel Hotel is written diagonally across the glass at the top half of the door. I stop and stare through the "O" which is level with my eyes. It is a black gothic "O." Through the oval letter I see across the street to the theater and the lighted marquee. The ticket booth is still empty.